The Marquess and the Earl

CHRISTINA DIANE

CHRISTINA
DIANE

The Marquess and the Earl

Unlikely Betrothal Series

Book Three

Copyright 2025 by Christina Diane

Edited by Emily Lawrence at Lawrence Editing

Cover Design by Erin at EDH Professionals

eBook ISBN: 978-1-964713-04-5

Paperback ISBN: 978-1-964713-13-7

Contents

Dedicated to those who shall never give up on fighting
for who and what they love.

Note to Readers

I am so delighted and honored that you have picked up my book! Before you dive in, I would like you to know that I write for the modern reader. My stories are character-driven, fast-paced, and spicy with fun dialogue. While I love the Regency era and exploring the social constructs for the time period, I don't focus on complete historical accuracy. I complete research and attempt to create the setting and behaviors that are close to what you would expect of the era, but sometimes the characters and story have minds of their own. I wouldn't want you to be disappointed if you want a setting, themes, and language that are entirely accurate. If that is really important to you, this book might not be for you. And I understand!

Historical stories are a form of escape and are a fantasy in their own right, and I aim to help bring you to a world that might look and feel very much like the Regency era with diverse, inclusive characters who are fun, sexy, and intriguing as they find their path to love.

If you are excited about hard-headed and swoonworthy gentlemen, spirited and passionate heroines, fun banter, high spice, and guaranteed happily ever afters, set in my interpretation of the Regency era, then I hope you will keep reading and escape into a world of passion, romance, and sharp tongues.

Content Warnings

While this particular series isn't heavy on content warnings (but high on spice), I do my best to capture things I think a concerned reader might wish to know. If you ever feel I missed something, please message me on socials or christinadiane@christinadianebooks.com and I will update this list to improve the reading experience for other readers. To prevent spoilers, you can find content warnings for all of my published books here: https://christinadianebooks.com/content-warnings/

Chapter 1

Nathaniel Baring, Marquess of Demming, watched the fields and trees pass outside of his carriage window. He still wasn't certain that he wished to attend the upcoming house party hosted by Viscount and Viscountess Ockham, but given that he was on the road to join the very event, it seemed the decision was made. His dear friend Juliana, a close friend of Viscountess Ockham, had him included on the guest list, even though she wouldn't be in attendance.

Juliana meant well, hoping that being with others might help him get over his lost love and not hide out in his country estate. Though the man who had captured his heart died over a year ago, he still wasn't certain if he could love anyone else with the same intensity. A carriage accident cost Nate a future that included love, and he'd spent the last year and a half grieving and coming to terms with the realization.

Nate hadn't been intimate with anyone since either, and a house party trapped with men who were vastly different from him would not help him remedy that desire even if he had it. He might not believe that love would come around again, but he didn't believe he wished to seek only his hand to meet his need for the rest of his days.

But it wouldn't be in the cards for the coming fortnight. He would be surrounded by ladies seeking marriage and widows seeking trysts, as well as the gentlemen who would look to partake in whichever of those selections were most appealing to them. It was the way of the world for men like him, living in a society where he could be sentenced to hang if anyone caught him in bed with a man. Yet, even with the risk, it had seemed inconsequential when he had the man he loved at his side.

There had only been one man since whom he thought might be intriguing, but he had misread the man's reaction to him. Fortunately, he figured it out before he made any intentions known towards the man, as that would have been disastrous. One couldn't simply walk into the room and ask the men which of them also enjoyed the other company of other men. Even if he could, it wouldn't mean that he would be attracted to them.

It made the entire business of finding someone that much harder. Which only made him wish he could bring his love back from the grave and continue the life they were building together.

Reducing the numbers to the size of a typical house party would only make his plight next to impossible, so he mentally prepared himself to flirt with a few of the ladies and listen to the men discuss all manner of inappropriate topics over their port. Surely he could survive a fortnight enjoying the same company. He liked the Ockhams when he met them at Juliana's wedding, so leaving with a few more close friendships would be worthwhile.

He sighed, almost convinced that he would enjoy his time at the house party and then retire to his country home again for a long while. Lonely and alone. Juliana was right. He needed to be around people more. Spending so much time on his own would eliminate any chance of love, or even someone to warm his bed, given he doubted that love was possible and a tryst was more probable.

The carriage pulled up into the circle drive of the large, opulent country home of Viscount Ockham. It wasn't as large as his own primary estate, but there was something charming about the light brick manor and beds of roses that lined the entire front of the home.

Once the carriage rolled to a stop, he emerged, not waiting for a footman to open the door for him. He was eager to stretch and move about on solid ground. Brushing the dust from the road off his coat and breeches, he started towards the stairs to greet his hosts.

"Lord Demming, how good of you to join us," Lady Ockham said, appearing at the top of the stairs with her husband by her side. They were a striking couple, and from what he knew of her ladyship, she was a force to be reckoned with.

When he reached the top of the stairs, he took her hand in his and bowed over it. "Thank you for the invitation, my lady."

Lord Ockham extended his hand to him, and Nate gave it a firm shake.

"Any friend of Juliana's is a friend of ours, of course," the lady said. "Perhaps you might even find the one who captures your heart while you are here." Her eyes twinkled at the notion. He wouldn't be surprised if she believed herself a bit of a matchmaker with her guest list, as most hostesses were rife to do.

"One can only hope," he lied. Juliana was the only one who knew of his secret, and she would never tell another soul, aside from her husband, who was surprisingly accepting of their friendship. The couple was a rare breed among the *ton,*for certain.

Lady Ockham looped her arm in Nate's and escorted him towards the entrance. Nate glanced back over his shoulder at her husband, who followed behind them, Lord Ockham's shoulders shaking from biting back his laughter.

"Is he laughing at me?" she asked.

Nate looked between them, unsure who was the most important to keep on his side.

Thankfully, Lord Ockham took it upon himself to respond. "You are just in your element, darling."

She waved him off and continued over the threshold of their home on Nate's arm. "I like you, Lord Demming."

"I like you, too, my lady," Nate replied, almost afraid to say anything otherwise. Although, he found he did like her very much. He also knew she was fiercely protective of her friends, which was admirable in their society.

"Demming, you will find it is best to succumb to whatever my wife has planned for you for the next fortnight," Ockham said, smirking at his wife. "She means well."

Nate was suddenly concerned about what matchmaking attempts she would execute and how he would avoid them.

"Don't worry, my lord," Lady Ockham said as if she read his thoughts. "I won't be forcing anyone on you.

Whom you spend the rest of your life with should be your own choice." She patted his arm. "I was selective in my guest list, seeking the most spirited, intriguing members of society. With maybe a few others sprinkled in to keep everyone on their toes. If love should bloom, all the better."

He smiled at her, relieved that she wouldn't attempt to see him leg shackled by the end of the party. A notion that, in his case, wouldn't be feasible. He wasn't certain he would ever wed, since he wouldn't do so without the woman knowing what she was getting herself into. And it would take an understanding woman to agree to such a match and keep his secrets.

"Baxter," Lady Ockham said, catching the man who appeared to be their butler. "Would you show Lord Demming to his chamber and ensure his trunks and valet are shown there as well?"

"Of course, my lady." The man motioned for Nate to follow him.

"Meet in the downstairs salon after you have refreshed yourself," Lady Ockham said before he departed. "I would like everyone downstairs by six, sharp. Dinner will be served shortly after."

Nate nodded and bowed to his hosts, then followed their butler up the stairs. A smile of satisfaction spread across his face as he entered his chamber, delighted with the room that would be his sanctuary for the next two weeks. He had an enormous four-poster bed, with a set of chairs and a settee before a fireplace. The fire hadn't been started yet, but he was certain his hosts would ensure it would be by the evening, given that they were approaching the season of cool fall evenings.

He dropped himself onto the settee and lay back, reminding himself he would have a pleasant time at the party and worry about the state of his love life, or lack thereof, at a later time.

Nate's trunks had arrived in his room, and his valet, Thompson, helped him to change into suitable dinner attire. Once he was freshly dressed and cologned, he departed his chamber. He was interested to see who from society would make the formidable Lady Ockham's guest list.

He spotted his hosts as soon as he entered the salon where the other guests had begun to gather.

"Good evening."

"Thank you for being prompt," Lady Ockham said, grinning at him. "Do mingle with the other guests. If you require introductions, just let me know."

"I see Onslow over there," Nate replied. "I believe I shall greet him next."

He at least knew most of the gentlemen in attendance from his days at Cambridge, and if not there, he had seen them at various events.

"Onslow, good to see you," Nate said, approaching him at the sideboard.

"You as well, Demming. Was it Ockham or his wife who talked you into attending?"

Nate laughed and poured himself a tumbler of brandy. "Neither. It was a mutual friend of ours, Juliana."

Onslow eyed him curiously, so Nate continued. "She seems to believe I need to get out of the house more, even though she is currently settled at home with her husband."

"These women are quite meddlesome," Onslow said, rolling his eyes.

"So which of our hosts roped you into attending?"

The man scoffed. "The viscountess, of course. She wouldn't take no for an answer. Although, I supposed I could think of worse ways to spend a fortnight."

"Does that mean you are looking at the young ladies in attendance in consideration of being the next Countess of Onslow?"

Onslow scoffed. "Not in the slightest. I'm going to continue enjoying bachelorhood as long as I can. What about you?"

"Same," Nate replied. "I hope to avoid the eager misses seeking the leg shackle."

Onslow held up his glass to him. "I'll toast to that."

Nate held up his glass in return. He knew Onslow from school well enough to know that the man didn't share Nate's interests. Onslow was attracted only to women, but for whatever reason, he fought the inevitable taking of a wife. It wasn't any of Nate's business, since he had no inclination to disclose his own reasons for doing the same.

"I promised our host I would mingle and meet the other guests," Nate said, "and she scares me."

"You had better do as she asked, that's for certain. I am sure we will hide together much of this fortnight."

Nate patted the man on the back and moved about the room with his drink in hand. A pretty blond woman moved out of his way and his breath caught when his gaze landed on the man in his line of sight. He had never seen the man and did not know who he was.

He appeared shorter than him by a couple of inches, which Nate liked. The man was broad-shouldered, with a trim waist. His hair was brown but with golden strands throughout, which were accentuated in the candlelit room. Nate couldn't see the man's eyes since he was glimpsing his profile, but he imagined they must be some kind of blue. At least that was what he hoped.

Nate noticed that the man spoke with a petite redhead. He would consider her quite pretty, with her red hair, adorable freckles, and heart-shaped face, but Nate imagined some of the *haute ton* considered her unfashionable. She smiled up at the man who took Nate's breath away, although her expression wasn't one of attraction. He wasn't certain that she was attached to the man, which was all the better for Nate.

Watching and observing people was something Nate had become very good at. It was a necessity in order to determine if a gentleman might return his interest. So far, he found nothing in the enticing man that might indicate he would return Nate's attraction, and he had every reason to believe the man was courting the redhead. What a lucky chit.

Before Nate could look away, the gentleman glanced in his direction and caught his gaze. He had been right about the eyes, as they were a deep sapphire blue. Something about them made him unable to look away. The man offered him a small grin and gave him a polite nod. He returned the gesture and then forced himself to turn away. He took a sip of his drink, attempting to appear nonchalant, even though his entire body had responded.

Hopefully, the man didn't find him strange after catching Nate watching him. Perhaps the gentleman would think he was curious about the lady in his presence. He wasn't fool enough to hope the man responded to him in the same way. Pining after a man who was only attracted to women was the definition of foolish for someone like him. It would lead nowhere. But it didn't mean he couldn't look and admire the man with no one else being the wiser.

"Are you having a pleasant time?" Lady Ockham asked, appearing next to him again.

"Indeed," he replied, taking another fortifying sip of his drink.

"Have you found anyone you weren't acquainted with?"

He pretended to look about the room before landing on the gentleman with the redhead, unable to stop himself from asking about the man who would haunt his dreams. "That gentleman over there and his lady friend. I haven't met them before."

She looked in the direction he indicated. "Oh, that is the Earl of Knox and Lady Lily Fairfax." She leaned closer as if she were about to tell him a secret. "Her father is hoping he will propose by the end of the house party. Lady Lily is a bit bookish and quiet in public, and her father wants her to wed a peer."

Nate's heart sank further with each of her words. He knew better than to allow himself even a small bit of hope.

"Come with me," Lady Ockham said. "I shall introduce you."

Chapter 2

George Knox, the Earl of Knox, was expected to do his duty to his title and his estates. He would marry, sire children, and ensure his estates prospered. That was what he had been raised to do. That was what his father had demanded of him. His father always demanded perfection in his only son. The sole heir to the earldom and the only one who could carry forth the family lines, else the estate would fall into the hands of some distant cousin. He had heard those words more times than he could count.

Even though his father had been gone for a few years now, he still heard the man's voice in his head. George wasn't like the other gentlemen. He had never enjoyed or excelled at sports. He wasn't all that great at riding a horse but did so passably. He didn't enjoy gambling or talking about bedding women, either. All faults for which his father hadn't hesitated to call out and chastise him about.

Only a perfect English gentleman would be acceptable, and that was what his father attempted to force him to be. George was made to practice his riding until his skill improved and forced to exercise to achieve the build his father expected in the Earl of Knox. His father even dragged him to brothels as soon as he was of age, encouraging him to "sow his oats" as the man put it. All of it was tiring, and not what George had wanted for his life. But the words of his father were still hard to overcome, even though the man no longer walked the earth.

He glanced down at the pretty young lady before him. She would suit his father's requirements if he were still here to check them off the list, one by one. Her hair color wasn't fashionable, but it suited her. She was also known to be on the quiet side, but his father would say that would make her a biddable wife who would do as she was told. Not that he had any desire to control a woman in such a way, or anyone, for that matter.

George did his best to listen to the young lady with feigned interest when he felt as if someone were watching him. The notion sent a chill through his body. He dared to turn his head to see if he was correct and found the most intriguing man watching him. At least he believed he was watching him. It was possible he could have been looking at Lady Lily.

But then he caught the man's gaze, and he couldn't look away. His green eyes shone like gems from where he stood across the room. His hair was a deep chestnut and looked as if it would be silky soft to the touch, and he was tall, with muscled broad shoulders. His chiseled jaw clenched, leaving George with no clue why the man was watching him.

He had been unable to look away, but thankfully, the man turned from him and greeted their host.

"Don't you agree, my lord?" Lady Lily said before him, attempting to capture his attention.

He swallowed. "Um…yes." Although, he hadn't the foggiest idea what he had just agreed to.

George's body shivered again, and he fought to keep from looking for the man with the piercing green eyes.

"My lord," their host said from his right. He hadn't even realized she had approached them. "My lady."

"Please allow me to make my friend, Lord Demming, known to you both. Marquess of Demming, this is the Earl of Knox and Lady Lily."

George looked at the man beside Lady Ockham and had to force himself to maintain a steady pace of breathing.

"It is a pleasure to meet you both," the man said coolly, his voice a rich baritone. He bowed over Lady Lily's hand and then gave George a respectful nod. He thought he detected something mischievous in the man's smile, and it did things to him. Things he didn't wish for others in the room to notice.

"You as well, my lord," George said, attempting to sound just as unfazed as the god in front of him appeared to be.

"Hopefully, I shall get to know both of you better during the house party, as I am sure we will partake in many of our hostess's activities together," the man said, appearing to speak more to George than to Lady Lily, which he knew was a ridiculous notion.

"I look forward to it, my lord," the young lady said from beside him. George was thankful for her response, allowing him a few extra moments to gather his wits.

Thankfully, dinner was announced, and everyone paired off to take their seats in the dining room. George did his best to focus on his meal and not look around the table. He was worried if he did, he would stare indefinitely at Lord Demming. He wasn't sure why he was so intrigued by the man, but he was completely infatuated with everything about him. If he thought he could ask someone about Demming without arousing suspicions, he would, if only so he could construct him as accurately as possible in his dreams.

George had known for a long time that he didn't have the same urges as most men of society. If he wasn't certain before his father took him to a brothel, his inability to rise to the occasion with a naked woman attempting to take him into her mouth only confirmed it. He paid the woman extra not to tell his father, or anyone else, for that matter.

He attempted the same act multiple times, determined to will his body to comply and enjoy the pleasures that a woman should be able to give his body, but it was no use. It certainly wasn't because he didn't want to come. He did very much, and he had from his own hand countless times.

George was almost certain he'd have a far different reaction to a man, given that his cock hardened from certain gentlemen who had caught his eye. He resorted to stroking his own shaft in response because he didn't dare to explore such a notion in actuality. It would be a risk to the title and his family's name.

He knew men like him existed, but it was well known that such a thing wasn't accepted in their society. Being with a man romantically was a crime punishable by death at the worst and social ruin at the best.

Given the bulge he sported in his breeches in the middle of dinner from the thought of the man seated a few guests down from him, it only continued to prove his theory, although the timing of the realization was unfortunate.

He had never been more thankful for the security of the large oak table and his napkin in his lap to shield him. He had the duration of dinner to control his urges and rid himself of the telling ridge between his thighs so he wouldn't embarrass himself in front of the entire party.

His father's words crept into his thoughts again, and that did the trick. The rest of dinner passed with him listening to the surrounding chatter and partaking in the conversation when he was spoken to.

The ladies departed, leaving the gentlemen to drink their port. George found himself even more uncomfortable in only the presence of men, always worried he might have a reaction to one of them. It happened from time to time when he noticed a gentleman he found appealing. His concern heightened with the intriguing Lord Demming so near to him.

Unable to help himself, he glanced over at Demming, who was in conversation with Ockham and Onslow. As if the man knew he was at the center of George's thoughts, Demming cast him a sideways glance from behind a sip of port. George thought he saw him grin, flashing a glimpse of his pearly white teeth before responding to something Onslow said.

"I hear you are courting one of the ladies in attendance," another man said from beside him. He turned his head, completely removing Demming from his line of sight, which was probably for the best.

"Perhaps," George said, responding to Viscount Alexander Callan. "Lady Lily's father put it around that we are courting, but I hardly know the lady. I merely discussed the notion with him."

"I suppose a house party is a splendid opportunity to remedy that. I hear there is to be a Pall Mall tournament tomorrow."

George fought the urge to groan. There was nothing he detested more than yard games. Well, that wasn't true. He could probably think of less appealing things, but he certainly hated them. He wasn't any good, and he could hear his father's disdain in his head when he could never hit the ball straight.

If he had any say in the matter, he would be a spectator, even if it meant he had to come down with some unexpected illness.

"Indeed," George replied, deciding that was the most agreeable response to give. He took a swig of his port, hoping that would end the conversation about such activities.

Finally, Ockham announced his desire to join the ladies. He was famous for the love match he had with his wife and spent very little time without her by his side. From what George knew of the lady, she was among the most spirited in society. He found he liked them both a lot. They seemed like the kind of people that if they knew of his interest in partners, or his assumed interest rather, they would be just as accepting. But he would never know for certain, so he would take that secret to his grave.

When he entered the room, he sought Lady Lily. It seemed like the appropriate thing to do. The upside to everyone in attendance believing that he was courting the woman was that the other young ladies steered clear of him, opting for gentlemen who appeared more available than he did. A small victory he was most grateful for.

"Are you enjoying the company of the other ladies?" he asked, reaching her side.

"I am, my lord," she replied. "It seems none of the gossips and more discerning members of the *ton* are in attendance."

With an overdramatic flair, he patted his chest. "Well, that is quite a relief."

She laughed at him. "You jest, but it is. I might even have an intellectual conversation without being called a bluestocking."

"What is it you are most interested in discussing?" he asked, finding that he was interested in her response.

"I mentioned earlier how I love reading and the theatre. So I always enjoy the opportunity to discuss those topics."

"And do you have a favorite play?"

"I can recite most of Shakespeare's plays by heart. I'm not certain I could select a favorite of his," she replied. She continued talking about it, but that nagging shiver captured George's attention.

He became distracted from their conversation when he noticed Demming by himself by the window, gazing into the night. He swirled his drink and then brought it to his lips. George took far too much notice of the way his mouth opened to pour the rich brown liquid into it.

"If you will excuse me," he said, almost certain he rudely interrupted whatever she was saying. "I am going to take in a bit of the night air."

He didn't wait for a response and started towards the double doors that led to the terrace, closing them behind him when he stepped out. Drawing a deep breath of the cool air, he hoped it would cool his heated skin.

"Hiding from your young lady?"

George closed his eyes, his entire body aware of who had appeared behind him. He stepped closer to the railing of the terrace if only to shield his lower body.

"Not at all, my lord," he said, glancing over his shoulder. "Just enjoying a bit of this beautiful evening." He glanced up as he had always enjoyed the beauty of the night sky. "The stars are on full display."

Demming joined him at the railing and looked up. "You are right about that. It's a perfect night for stargazing. Oh look, a shooting star."

"Am I to believe that you make wishes on stars?" George would find it hard to believe that a man of Demming's looks and stature would do something so frivolous.

Demming turned his head to look at him. "Indeed, I do."

"Perhaps I should make a wish that I can get out of playing Pall Mall tomorrow."

Demming laughed. "Not a fan, I take it?"

George shook his head. "Hate isn't a strong enough word."

"Well, I shall do my best to help you avoid it, even if I must sacrifice myself to ensure no young lady is without a partner."

George grinned at him. "Then I shall be in your debt."

He waved him off. "Not at all. You can just cheer me on from the sidelines."

"You have a deal," George said.

Demming extended his hand for them to shake on it. George hesitated but grabbed it. The electricity from the man's touch reached every cell in his body. He had never had a stronger urge to lean forward and press his lips to another's as he did to the full pout of the handsome man before him.

He feared he had held the man's hand too long and pulled away. "I should return. Lady Lily might wonder where I have gotten off to."

Given his lack of composure and his telltale physical reaction to Lord Demming, he bypassed the salon and retired to his chamber for the evening. He'd need to have far better control over himself tomorrow. Lord Demming was not for him.

Chapter 3

Sleep hadn't come easy for Nate the previous evening. The connection he felt between him and Lord Knox drove him to distraction. He retraced and dissected every piece of their conversation and the man's reaction to him, hoping he wasn't reading into the attraction he believed the man might have for him. He knew for certain he hadn't experienced such intensity for another in quite a long time.

He was the kind of man who enjoyed romance, and something more than casual interactions with men, with the right man. It was difficult in their society, and sometimes trysts and flings were all that could be afforded.

Part of him felt guilty for the attraction and intrigue he had for another man, but he knew his dear departed love would want him to be happy. Juliana reminded him of the same repeatedly. Deep down, he knew he must move on at some point, but if he found someone he could consider giving his heart to again, it scared him. Even more so was the fact that he wasn't yet certain if the man was even interested in him. He could have read him all wrong, which wouldn't do at all.

He threw the covers back and set about readying himself for the day. Thompson knocked on the door a few moments later to help him dress. Once he was freshly shaved and donning a perfectly tailored coat and breeches, he departed to join the rest of the party in the breakfast room.

Upon exiting his room, the door next to his own opened, and Knox emerged. If Nate had known that the man who consumed his thoughts all evening was sleeping just next door to him, sleep would have evaded him completely. He wasn't certain how he would manage later that evening, other than from sheer exhaustion.

"Good morning," he said, noting the surprised reaction from Knox as well.

"Good day, my lord."

The pair fell in step beside each other.

"We still have our deal. I shall protect you from yard games," Nate said, assessing the man's response.

Knox shook his head and laughed. "Do you always play the part of the hero?"

Nate shrugged. "For some. Depends on who you ask." He hoped the man might give him anything that would be a sign that he was interested in more than polite, gentlemanly friendship. With any luck, much more.

But while Knox was engaging and attentive to him, Nate still wasn't sure.

When they arrived at the breakfast room, many other guests were already there. They each made their plates at the sideboard, and he decided to be bold and take a seat right beside where Knox sat. A hint of sandalwood from the soap Knox must have used wafted in Nate's direction, and he fought not to close his eyes at the sensation.

He imagined that he might find a reason to press his thigh against Knox's or to lean closer, if only to ascertain if it would garner a reaction. But he couldn't do such a thing in the middle of the breakfast room, with the rest of the guests bearing witness. That was a gamble a man in his position could never take without the certainty of how the attention would be received.

Lady Lily was seated on the other side of Knox, and she took up most of the man's attention. Nate noted that Knox didn't seem to flirt with her or attempt to win her to his suit, but it wasn't a definitive conclusion as to whether the man might have an interest in him.

Nate spent most of breakfast staring at his plate and listening to their conversation, still seeking any clues about the mysterious man who captured his attention.

Once everyone had finished with their breakfast, Lady Ockham encouraged them to move outdoors. The entire party did as she directed, and soon everyone stood in a circle around her.

"I want everyone to pair off in teams for a game of Pall Mall, and there will be a prize for the winning team."

Nate held back and waited to see which young lady might need a partner. He typically preferred to partner with ladies who struggled to find partners otherwise. He took the same approach in ballrooms. Nate did his best to help build the confidence of the overlooked young ladies, while not encouraging them to set their cap at him.

He caught Knox's gaze and nodded towards the area that had been set up for the spectators. Knox rewarded him with a grin and backed away. Nate noticed that Miss Watson was without a partner. She was the daughter of a baron and commonly pretty. He would assume she was shy, given she just had her first season out in society.

"Miss Watson, might you be willing to partner with me?"

She giggled. "I would be delighted."

He stood beside her while the rest of the pairings lined up to begin the game.

The game wasn't usually played with partners, but Nate assumed that Lady Ockham altered the game to encourage couples to pair off and spend time together. They would take turns hitting the same ball, which would mean he would be at the mercy of the skill of Miss Watson to determine if they might have a chance at besting their opponents.

When it was their turn, he motioned for Miss Watson to go first. From the first hit, he knew they were going to be in for a long game, and it was unlikely they would win. At least that would take the pressure off, and he could focus more of his attention on the man who watched from the sidelines.

When their turn came again, Nick stepped up to the ball. He stretched and flexed, putting on a show, then took his hit, quick and smooth, sending the ball through the first wicket.

He glanced over at the sidelines to see if Knox had been watching and found him beaming and clapping along with the other spectators. Nate caught his gaze and gave him a nod. He could have sworn that the man smiled wider, but it might have been his imagination.

Each time Nate took his turn, he fell into a similar cadence. He did what he could to encourage the man to take notice of him and watched to see if he did. They had fallen behind after a few horrendous plays from Miss

Watson, but Nate didn't care. He found he was enjoying the game. The one on the field, as well as the one he played with the man on the sidelines.

Hours later, when the game was over, Lady Eliza and Lord Irvine were declared the winners and awarded their prizes. The group dispersed to roam the grounds, take naps, tend to correspondence, and whatever else they wished to do until a late luncheon would be served on the terrace.

Nate thanked Miss Watson for partnering with him and took off for the sidelines where Knox still watched him.

"You held up your end of the bargain," Nate said to him. "I only apologize that your cheering efforts didn't produce a win."

Knox grinned and Nate's heart beat harder. "That hardly seemed to be any fault of yours. You play splendidly."

"I thought of exploring Ockham's library. Would you care to join me?" Nate asked. The man's response would be telling, and perhaps if he could get him alone, he might determine once and for all if the attraction was one-sided.

"I would enjoy that. I hear he has quite the collection."

Nate fought not to smile too wide as it wasn't a confirmation, but it gave him a bit more hope.

The pair crossed the yard and ascended the steps of the terrace. Nate navigated them to where he understood the private library to be. Once they reached the door, he motioned for Knox to enter first. Nate followed and closed the door behind them once he realized they were alone.

He swallowed hard and turned towards where Knox was. The man was skimming various titles along the shelves. He glanced at Nate and said, "There are so many wonderful editions."

Nate clasped his hands behind his back and watched. He thought he noticed a familiar bulge in the man's breeches, but then Knox turned to look at shelves behind him. Nate pushed aside the thoughts that staring at the man's backside ignited within him as it wouldn't do to lose himself.

Knox reached for a book above his head and struggled to grab it. Nate was only about two inches or so taller than him, but it would be enough. "Allow me." He came up behind Knox and reached for the book, his front pressed against the man's bottom, his cock aware of the proximity. He grabbed the book and backed away to hand it to him.

Knox turned to grab the book, and Nate's gaze dropped to the man's crotch, which tested the integrity of the buttons that held his falls in place. Nate grinned and thanked the stars that his instincts had been right.

The man noticed where Nate had focused and hurried to place the book in front of himself. "My lord, I, uh, it's not…"

"You have nothing to be embarrassed about," Nate said softly. "Nor do you need to hide your attraction from me. Anything you feel is quite all right."

Knox swallowed hard, and his neck was flushed. Nate hadn't been with countless men, but with the experience he did have, he suspected from the uneasiness in his reaction that Knox didn't have any experience with men. Or he hadn't glanced between Nate's thighs to notice that he sported the same bulge and returned his attraction.

Nate turned away and started towards the door.

"My lord," Knox called out, trepidation in his voice, "please don't go."

Nate turned the lock on the door and turned back to face him.

"I just didn't wish for anyone to enter."

Knox nodded in understanding and released a sigh of relief, his eyelids heavy with desire. Nate crossed the room back to him. He stepped close and ran his knuckles along the man's jaw, pleased that he didn't flinch or back away.

"Have you ever been kissed by a man?" Nate asked, his voice low and gravelly.

Knox swallowed again and shook his head.

"Would you like for me to kiss you?"

"Yes," he said, but it came out more of a sigh than a word.

Nate shifted his knuckles under the man's jaw and tilted his chin up to him, then lowered his lips to press them against his. Knox shifted his hands to clasp Nate's shoulders, and Nate responded by wrapping his arm around the man's waist and pulling him against his body. He deepened the kiss, running his tongue at the seam of Knox's lips until he opened for him, allowing him to slip his tongue inside. He wasn't certain that anything had ever tasted as good.

He massaged his tongue harder against Knox's, and the man's hand found its way into Nate's hair, which caused him to moan into their kiss. The reaction ignited something in Knox, and he took more control of the kiss, their tongues warring and their bodies pressed together. Nate clasped the man's tight bottom and pulled him harder against his aching cock.

Knox broke the kiss. "May I touch you?" he asked.

Nate grinned and placed a light kiss on his lips. "You can touch me anywhere you like. You needn't ask."

Knox grinned at him and licked his lips. The action sent electric surges straight to Nate's cock. The man ran his hands down Nate's body until he reached his falls. Each move of the man's hand as he worked the buttons drove Nate further into madness. His cock sprang to life between them and Knox gripped it with his hand, lazily stroking it.

"That feels so good," Nate whispered, slowly rocking his hips against the man's hand. "Please tell me I can touch you."

Knox grinned at him. "You needn't ask."

Nate made quick work of unbuttoning the man's falls, requiring no further invitation, and in a matter of moments, he gripped the rock-hard cock of the man before him.

Nate lowered his lips again and swept his tongue into Knox's mouth, tasting the tea with honey on his breath. He matched the pace of his tongue's movements to that of his hand before he backed Knox towards the settee in the study, not breaking their kiss. When the back of the man's legs reached the settee, he urged him to sit.

He knelt before him, positioning himself between his legs, and massaged his thighs as he looked up at him. "Has anyone sucked your cock before?" Nate asked, looking up at him.

Knox reached out and cupped Nate's cheeks, running his hands behind his head into his hair, capturing his gaze. "Not by a man."

Something about knowing he would be the first man to introduce Knox to such things only made the moment more thrilling. He lowered his mouth over the man's cock, sucking inch after inch into his mouth until he took the entire thing. Knox bucked and moaned, gripping Nate's head as he licked and sucked his thick shaft.

Nate slipped his hand between his own legs and stroked himself to the same pace he set for moving his mouth up and down on Knox's cock. After several hard sucks, Nate was rewarded for his efforts when his mouth filled with warm proof and ragged pants and groans from Knox. He swallowed down and sucked every drop until Knox stilled, fighting to catch his breath.

Nate continued to stroke himself, looking up at Knox, sated and watching him.

"Please, let me," Knox pleaded. "I have never made anyone, besides myself, come before."

Nate almost spent at the words but ceased his movements and brought himself to stand before the irresistible man. "I'll spend no matter what you use, your hand or your mouth. Your choice. Whatever you wish."

Knox gripped the cock before him, still seated, so he was at eye level with Nate's large shaft. He made a fist around it and stroked it with his hand. Nate moved his hips to push himself into Knox's hand, imagining what it might feel like if the man was bent over before him. Perhaps that would occur soon enough. Given Knox's inexperience, he mustn't rush things, but a man could dream.

The man's warm tongue brushed the end of Nate's cock, causing him to cry out. "Oh, fuck."

It had been so long since he had been touched by anyone but his own hand, and the experience proved to be intoxicating.

Knox must have liked the outburst because he sucked in more of Nate's shaft, still stroking the base. The man was a quick study. He sucked harder, and Nate came undone, thrusting himself against the man's mouth and fist.

"I'm going to…" He thought to warn the man in case he wasn't ready for the warm eruption that was inevitably coming. Knox responded by sucking hard, and Nate rocked his hips one more time, and his balls tightened as he released everything he had onto the man's willing tongue.

Knox must have swallowed it all and fell back against the settee, looking up at Nate. Nate wasn't certain he had ever seen anything more attractive than the sight of that perfect man sated and gazing up at him, having just swallowed everything he gave him. He wasn't certain what he saw in Knox's eyes, but it took Nate's ragged breath away. He hadn't been hopeful he might find someone he even wanted to feel a deeper affection with until Knox looked up at him that way.

Drawing a deep breath to return the air to his lungs, Nate tucked himself back inside his falls and buttoned them. They had been quite fortunate that no one had knocked on the door or attempted to enter. Nate pulled Knox to stand and buttoned his falls back for him, too. The action felt intimate, and Nate found he liked it. Too much. As much as he had been scared and saddled with guilt over the notion of finding such intimacy with someone else, he craved it with this man.

"My lord," Knox started before Nate cut him off.

"Nate, please. I believe we can dispense with the formalities."

He nodded. "I am George."

"George," Nate said, trying it out on his lips.

"Nate, should we discuss what just occurred?"

Nate placed a quick kiss on George's lips to reassure him. "Yes, but not here. We have been hidden away in here for far too long. We shall have a chance again soon."

George nodded, biting his bottom lip.

Unable to resist, Nate kissed him again and then soothed the place that George had just bit with his tongue. "You were perfect, and I very much want to get to know each other better. We just have to be careful."

That seemed to ease George's worried expression. Nate kissed him one more time, hoping the man wouldn't worry for a second that Nate had taken pleasure from him with no further intention. That couldn't be further from the truth.

Chapter 4

George's head spun after what had occurred between him and Nate in the library. Disbelief consumed him as he pondered how he had summoned the courage to be so bold and how someone as handsome and perfect as Nate could find him desirable. It had been the most sensual and pleasurable experience of his life. He feared that once would never be enough now that he was aware of what pleasure at the hands—and mouth—of another man felt like. Not just another man. Nate.

He fought a silly grin from referring to him by his given name. It was probably short for Nathaniel, which suited such a strong, athletic man. He pushed his thoughts aside as he couldn't allow himself to fall for the man. They had no longstanding future together. He must wed a woman and secure his title. That was what he was born to do. His father's words reverberated in his mind, reminding him of such responsibility.

As much as he knew he should avoid being in Nate's presence and push aside every bit of the reaction he had to the man, he knew with every shiver of his body that he wouldn't. If this was the only chance he had in life to experience such pleasure and passion, he should take it. He would certainly not find it in a marriage that befitted the expectations of society.

After they departed the library, they parted ways. It wouldn't do for them to be seen together so frequently that they raised suspicion, especially given that they weren't known to each other before they had arrived. They could enjoy some of the activities in the same circles and share polite conversation, but they could not be seen in each other's company constantly. George might not know much about how this sort of thing worked, but he was certain of that much.

Nate said they would speak more later, so he only hoped they might be alone together. He wished to learn more about him and to better understand what Nate's situation was. Had he always been attracted to men? Given the man's experience and confidence with such matters, George wasn't naïve enough to believe that had been his first time. The thought didn't plague him with jealousy. Well, perhaps a bit, but he was curious to learn more about the man who had captured his every thought.

"I don't think you are listening to me at all," Lady Lily said, seated on the settee beside him.

George shook off his thoughts and glanced at her. "What? Oh, my sincere apologies. Woolgathering, I suppose."

She assessed him but didn't seem angry. "You needn't feel pressured to ask for my hand, even if my father should say otherwise."

"I don't, my lady. I assure you. I am just enjoying getting to know you better." That last part wasn't a lie. He enjoyed the young lady, just not in the way her father hoped and not as much as he enjoyed Nate.

"Your wandering thoughts would suggest otherwise," she said, smirking at him. She had a bit of spirit in her, hidden by the bluestocking persona that society had applied to her.

The corners of his lips curved to form a playful smile. "Well, may I tell you a secret?" he asked, leaning just a bit closer when she eyed him curiously. "I'm not very good at this."

She laughed and covered her mouth when a group standing nearby took notice. "We have that in common, my lord."

"Well, that's a start," he said. It was indeed something. At least he was feeling a bit more comfortable in the lady's presence.

He stayed by her side for the rest of the afternoon. He forced Nate from his mind and only allowed him to cloud his thoughts every few minutes, as opposed to every thought. It aided in improving his conversation skills with Lady Lily. She was the kind of woman he would like to be friends with. If he must succumb to the weight of his responsibilities, there were certainly worse options to consider.

But even knowing that, something held him back from proposing and getting it over with. He had several more days, so why rush things? Because once he did, he wouldn't be able to go back on it, so he had better be certain before he took that next step towards being the earl that society, and his father, expected him to be.

George was acutely aware of Nate's presence through-out dinner. They had been seated across from each other, so he had to force himself not to stare at him and risk anyone else taking notice. Especially when his thoughts weren't of a pure nature.

Nate gave him a small smile once when their gazes caught but shifted his focus to Lady Juliet sitting to his left. The way he flirted and chatted with the pretty young lady left George with more questions. Perhaps Nate was also attracted to women. The notion seemed reasonable enough, even though it didn't appear to be the case for himself. Perhaps Nate intended to offer for the lady. He was a marquess, after all. He was in the same position as George and would need to take a wife.

George sighed to himself, thinking of them each married and hidden away in their respective country homes. He'd likely never see the man again after the house party, especially since George didn't prefer to attend all the events of the London season.

He felt that awareness of being watched and glanced at Nate, who was staring back at him, a concerned expression written on his features. Nate must have observed George's mental turmoil. George mentally reminded himself that he'd have to take greater care to mask his emotions and expressions. He gave Nate a small smile, hoping to put the man's mind at ease, and then refocused his attention on his plate.

Lady Lily hadn't been seated next to him that evening, and with the ladies on each side of him already engaged in conversation, George could continue to stare at his plate and avoid the polite niceties. He forked a bite of venison into his mouth and tamped down the feelings he couldn't name.

When the ladies departed so the gentlemen could converse over their port, George ensured he wasn't anywhere near Nate. He joined in a conversation about some of the upcoming races. He wasn't much of a gambler, but he at least enjoyed attending the events, so the conversation came easy and aided in distracting himself from thoughts of Nate, at least for a few moments.

The gentlemen rejoined the ladies in the salon to find that their hostess had set up a few tables for guests to partake in card games. George enjoyed such games, but his mind wasn't right for it that evening. He went to the sideboard, got himself a healthy pour of brandy, and started for the terrace. Perhaps if he was missing when everyone paired off for the games, he wouldn't get roped into playing.

He rested his forearms on the railing and looked out across the yard. He took a large gulp of his drink and then resumed his position. Losing himself in his thoughts, he didn't hear Nate approach.

"Something troubling you?"

George swirled his drink and took another sip, appreciating the warmth and burn as it moved down his throat. "Just thinking."

"About me, I hope," the devilish man said.

George glanced over at him at that, his heart almost coming to a complete stop at the way the wind lightly tousled Nate's hair and the way the light from the moon created shadows on his face, which only made him more irresistible. If George didn't care so much about them being seen and the devastation it would bring down upon both of them, he would toss his glass over the railing and capture the man's lips and tongue.

Instead, he took another sip of his drink. "Indeed."

"Will you meet me tonight?"

George glanced at him again. "Meet you?"

Nate nodded. "Meet me just over there at midnight."

He looked to where Nate pointed, and it was just off the terrace to the side of the house. George shifted his attention back to Nate. "I have a lot of questions," George said, suddenly feeling shy and glancing at his feet. He wanted to better understand himself and to know Nate better. And after what had occurred between them, he also wanted to know more about what could occur between men like them.

Nate shifted his hand to the other side of the railing and brushed his fingers along George's wrist, where no one could see.

"Just meet me, and I will tell you anything you wish to know."

"I'll be there," George replied.

"Midnight," Nate reminded.

"Midnight."

Nate departed, leaving George alone on the terrace again. He downed the rest of his brandy. The next few hours would surely be the longest of his life.

Around ten minutes until midnight, George quietly exited his room. He was half curious if he might encounter Nate as he made his way to their meeting place, given that Nate's room was next door to his own. It wouldn't do for them to be caught together wandering the house in the middle of the night. Given the trysts that occurred at such events, it wouldn't be out of the realm of possibility to encounter others who intended to spend the night in a different chamber.

He crept down the stairs and passed through the salon. Trying his best to stay in the shadows as much as possible, he was fortunate that he didn't encounter anyone by the time he reached the terrace. He descended the stairs and then leaned against the house, under the cover of darkness. His heart raced, and he stretched his arms out to his sides, flattening his palms against the cool brick to steady himself.

George wasn't sure what the night would hold, but he hoped he might at least get to kiss Nate again.

"I'm glad you made it," Nate whispered, startling him.

"I told you I would meet you," George replied, trying to get control of his quickened breathing, partly from being startled and partly because of the man in front of him.

Before George could say or think anything else, Nate cupped his cheek and brushed his full lips against George's. George wrapped his arms around Nate's waist and returned the kiss, slipping his tongue inside the man's mouth to explore and taste every bit of him.

After several minutes, Nate broke the kiss and rested his forehead against George's. "Follow me."

Nate turned and started walking towards a thick group of trees. He carried a small satchel.

"Wait, where are we going?" George whispered after him.

If Nate heard him, he didn't acknowledge him and kept moving to the line of trees and then crossed between them. George followed behind him. He hadn't thought they would go traipsing through the woods, but it didn't stop him from following as closely as he could. He was thankful he still donned his full dinner kit since it was a crisp evening.

Once they cleared the trees, there was a small open field. It was a large circle clearing with enough tree cover that no one could see them from the house if they looked out their windows.

"Help me with this," Nate called out to him.

George saw the blanket he had pulled from his satchel. Nate handed him one side of it and instructed him to help him spread it out. Once it was flat against the grass, Nate kneeled on it before shifting to sit. He patted the space beside him on the blanket, and George followed suit. He wasn't sure what he had expected when he agreed to meet, but it certainly wasn't the scene before him. It was even better.

Nate pulled an open bottle of wine from his satchel and a loaf of bread.

"We will have to drink directly from the bottle, and all I could grab was this loaf of bread, so it wasn't exactly the picnic I would have liked to have packed," Nate said, handing George the bottle.

George took a swig and handed it back to him. "This is really thoughtful, Nate."

"I thought we might watch the stars together," Nate said, grinning at him.

George swallowed the emotion that bubbled far too close to the surface. He had met no one as kind or romantic, let alone someone who caused his heart to beat faster than it ever had before, not that he could allow himself to admit such a thing.

"I'd like that very much," George whispered.

Nate set the bottle of wine to the side and laid the bread on top of the satchel. He lay flat on his back. "Come, lie with me."

George shivered, feeling far more than he should have for the man. Unable to resist, he lay beside him, their heads only a few inches apart. Nate clasped George's hand and laced their fingers together, and the electricity from Nate's fingers rubbing against his own sent shivers through George's entire body.

They lay together in silence for a few moments, staring up at the millions of stars in the sky. It was a clear night, making the stars appear even brighter. George also saw himself more clearly than he ever had before and he longed to better understand what it all meant.

George drew a deep breath, searching for the words to ask Nate all his questions. He turned his head to look at him, mesmerized by the handsome man's profile and the steady rise and fall of his chest. George turned on his side to face him.

"Have you always," he started, breaking the silence. He paused, landing on the way he wished to ask his question before continuing, "Fancied men?"

Nate turned his head to look at him, remaining on his back with their hands still clasped. "I'm not certain. I guess so. It just feels like the most normal thing in the world to me, so I don't really question it."

"But how did you know? When did you…" George's voice trailed off. He was certain that if Nate could see him better, he'd find that George's skin had turned to a dark shade of red.

"Are you trying to ask me about the first time I was with a man?" Nate asked.

George nodded, relieved that Nate understood his meaning. "Yes."

"How much do you want to know?"

George thought about his question before answering. "Everything."

"When I was eight-and-ten, just before I was to start at Cambridge, I happened upon an attractive footman in our household changing clothes in a closet. Something in the kitchen had spilled and made a mess. His back was to me, and I couldn't look away. I hadn't been certain at that point, but I'd suspected I might fancy men from other reactions I'd had. When he turned around, I was frozen in place in the doorway. My attraction was obvious, if you understand what I'm saying, and he noticed."

Nate paused, and George nodded, urging him to continue.

"I was so embarrassed and afraid he would tell others in the household, or my father, so I tried to avoid the man until I left for school. But he sought me out, apparently having experienced a similar attraction. That was the first time that a man used his mouth on my cock. Well, anyone, actually."

Nate squeezed George's hand, searching his face in the dark. "Do you wish to hear more, or is that enough?" he asked.

"Tell me all of it," George replied. He wanted to understand more than anything, especially if it would serve to enlighten him about the ways that intimacy occurred between men.

"I started university after that. I wasn't certain what it all meant, and I noticed attraction to other men but never acted on it. When I returned home for holiday break, the footman snuck into my chamber one evening and encouraged me to…well, to insert my cock into his arse."

George knew that men inserted themselves inside women when they coupled but hadn't considered that the arse might be pleasurable. If the reaction from his cock was any indication, the mental image of Nate doing such a thing to him would be quite intriguing, indeed.

"Did you enjoy doing so?" George asked, almost certain he already knew the answer.

"If I am honest, I did so every day while on holiday, sometimes twice, until I returned to school."

"Did you love him?" George asked, no hint of jealousy in his tone.

Nate laughed and waved him off. "No. I was a green lad then and was just glad to dip my prick into something. I wasn't certain how much gender played a factor at that point, or if I enjoyed the climax it gave me. A group of the guys at school decided to visit a brothel. I paid for my time with a woman and we went into a private room. I was able to finish, but it wasn't as satisfying. I accepted then that I preferred men, and it was just who I was. I decided I'd deal with the rest as it came, as it were."

"And then you fucked a lot of other men?" This time there was a bit more of a jealous edge, which George immediately regretted.

Nate turned on his side now to face him. "No, actually. I admittedly continued to use the willing footman to tend to my needs when I wasn't away at school, but in my last year at Cambridge, I met someone. And him…I loved."

George hated the pain in Nate's expression and used his thumb to smooth Nate's furrowed brow. George swallowed hard, wanting to know more, but not wanting to cause the man any more pain. Or himself, if he were honest, but he had to ask. "Where is he now?"

"He died," Nate said, offering no more information, and George decided not to pry any further.

"I'm sorry."

Nate nodded but said nothing.

The silence hung between them for a few moments. There was so much more to Nate than George might have realized, and it endeared him to the man even more. His feelings grew stronger with every minute spent in his presence, and he knew he was playing with fire.

"What about you?" Nate asked, breaking through George's thoughts. "How did it happen for you?"

George released an uncomfortable chuckle. "Well, you already know that I don't have any experience."

"When did you first realize you looked at men differently than our society tells you that you should?"

"I was maybe seven-and-ten or somewhere around there. From my chamber window, there was a stream where the servants would bathe in the summer. One day, I noticed one of the grooms, who was particularly fit, removed his clothing and entered the stream naked. Before I knew it, my cock was in my hand, and my seed soiled a handkerchief. I fisted myself at the window more times than I care to admit."

"So you like a muscled man, I see?" Nate asked, teasing him.

"It's embarrassing to think back on." George couldn't believe he had shared such a private experience with another person, but Nate wasn't just another person to him. Not in the slightest.

Nate leaned forward and pressed his lips to George's for a quick, soft kiss. "It's not at all. You don't think I've fucked my own hand more times than I can count?"

The mental image that gave George stirred a reaction in him, and his cock became aware of just how close Nate was to him at that moment.

"Have you bedded a woman?" Nate asked, only slightly taking the edge off the strain of George's breeches.

"I tried, but I'm not like you," George replied.

"What do you mean?"

"I couldn't do it. I couldn't finish. I couldn't even really start." He hung his head as if it were something he should be ashamed of. "I tried several times."

Nate placed his knuckles under his chin and lifted George's head so he looked into his eyes. "Hey, I don't care what anyone else says. It doesn't matter. Attraction isn't always this or that, and sometimes it is. If you only want to be with a man in that way, that's what is right for you."

Understanding washed over George, and he had never felt better about who he was than at that moment under the stars with the man before him. Before he could stop himself, George shifted on top of him, pushing Nate onto his back, and straddled his hips. George leaned down to press hungry kisses against his lips. Nate wrapped his arms around him and kissed him back, matching his intensity.

George broke the kiss. "I want you, Nate."

Nate cupped his cheeks and kissed his forehead. "And I want you, more than anything. I never thought I might even dream to have this kind of attraction for another again, and it's wonderful." He paused and stared into George's eyes. "That's why I will do nothing more than kiss you tonight. I didn't bring you out here to seduce you. I planned this to spend time with you and learn everything I could about you, and hope that you might wish to learn more about me."

George contemplated what he said. He wasn't certain anyone had ever shown him such care. His father certainly hadn't. At least not the care he needed. The experience was unlike anything he might have ever thought to have with another person, and his heart swelled with such intensity that it might burst from his chest. He shifted his hips, adjusting himself from how his cock throbbed and ached.

Appearing to notice George's discomfort, Nate took George's hand and placed it on the steel bulge within his breeches. "In case you doubt my words, there is your proof. If you wish to be intimate tomorrow when you aren't entranced by the romance of the evening, I will do whatever you request of me."

Nate released George's hand and then George shifted so he lay beside him again, clasping their hands and continuing to watch the stars. They talked for a couple more hours. George told Nate all about how his father had treated him and how nothing was more important to the man than the earldom. Nate said he might have taken George's father to task on his behalf if the man were still alive.

Nate shared some details of his childhood and his parents. His father had also passed, but his mother was still alive. Nate said he wondered if she might suspect his preference for men but indicated that she had said nothing about it if so.

They talked about their favorite colors, foods, ice flavors from Gunter's, songs, and anything else they could think of. Nate teased George about being an Oxford man, since he had attended Cambridge.

The comfort they found with each other was as if they had known each other for years. George hated for it to end. As mad and fast as it was, one thing was for certain. He was in love. He wasn't certain in which moment it had happened, but without question, Nate was what had been missing from his life.

"Look, a shooting star!" Nate exclaimed. "Make a wish."

George watched as Nate closed his eyes, and he did the same. He wished silently to himself that the perfect man beside him might love him one day.

"What did you wish for?" George asked.

Nate shook his head. "I can't tell you. Or else it might not come true."

George grinned at him. He loved how romantic Nate could be. In truth, he already cared deeply about Nate.

"We better get back and try to get a few hours of sleep," Nate said.

"You are probably right."

"I usually am," Nate teased.

They packed the blanket and empty wine bottle into the satchel and set off together, hand in hand. Once they reached the side of the house, Nate pulled George against him, then placed several light kisses along his lips and jaw. "Go up first. I'll follow after several minutes."

"Nate?"

"Yes, handsome?"

George stared into his eyes, wanting to tell Nate how he felt about him. To end their perfect evening with a declaration of his affection. His body trembled, afraid to be vulnerable, but knowing it was true.

"I—" He swallowed hard. "What I mean to say is that I…well…I am feeling things for you."

Nate kissed George's brow.

"Me too," Nate said, cupping his cheek with his hand.

"You do?" George asked, a tear escaping down his cheek.

"I do, and it's frightening. I'm uncertain what to think about it."

George nodded in agreement. That was an understatement. He did not know what it meant for them, or how a future might work. Or if they would even try to have a future after the house party. Those were problems for tomorrow, perhaps even next week. They would have to see how the next several days unfolded.

George kissed him again until Nate broke the kiss. "Go on," Nate urged. "Get some sleep. I'll see you at breakfast."

Reluctant to leave Nate, George did as he said and crept back up the terrace and didn't stop until he reached his chamber. Once on the other side of his door, he leaned against it, his heart pounding at the events of the evening.

He felt his entire world had changed within a matter of a couple of days, and he wasn't certain what it would all mean. But he smiled because Nate had feelings for him, too.

Chapter 5

Nate had collapsed across his bed the previous evening. He fell asleep with a smile fixed on his face and woke up with the same smile. Even though it was sudden and quick, he wasn't certain how he had been fortunate enough to find such a strong connection twice in his life, but he didn't wish to take a moment of it for granted.

He almost knocked on George's door and spent the night with him, but he reminded himself of the need to put some space between their emotional declarations and the physical aspects of being together. At least for one evening. After all that they had shared with each other, and better understanding the confusion George had lived with for much of his life, Nate knew George deserved unconditional love and affection. And not just the physical kind, although that would come quickly, so to speak, given how much they both wanted it.

Perhaps they could break away from the riding party and find a place where they could be alone. That might be better than having to maintain hushed whispers to keep from being found out. At least for George's first time.

Nate grabbed a few things he thought they might need, then wrapped them up in the sheet that had been in his satchel before placing the sheet back inside. A knock sounded at the door, and he allowed Thompson to enter to help him dress. While he readied himself for the day, he came up with a plan for how they would separate from the group without raising suspicion.

Once he was dressed, he left the satchel just inside his chamber and departed to join the others in the breakfast room. He glanced at George's door, wondering if he was inside or if he was already downstairs. Nate continued walking, knowing he would have his answer soon enough and could put the plan into action.

As soon as he reached the roar of the conversation where breakfast was served, he immediately saw George seated next to Lady Lily. He was freshly shaven, and Nate hid his frown. Although he still thought the man delectable, he preferred him with a bit of scruff. Hopefully, they might get away together somewhere for several days after the house party and forgo shaving. Nate enjoyed the roughness from the shadow of a beard that George sported the previous evening.

He'd have to quit thinking about it, at least until he was seated. Nate made several selections from the sideboard and took a seat across from George and Lady Lily.

"Good morning, my lady," he said, opting to greet the young lady before greeting the person he cared the most about in the world. He hated he had to do so and be so mindful of their interactions. Perhaps they'd see a day in their society where that wasn't the case.

"Good morning, Lord Demming," she said, offering him a kind smile. "Are you joining the ride today?"

"I am, my lady." He shifted his focus to George, his heart pounding when their eyes met. "And what about you, Lord Knox?"

"I believe I shall," he replied.

Breakfast passed with various polite conversations and the other guests confirming who would attend the group ride and picnic by the pond. Not long after breakfast, everyone congregated at the stables and each guest claimed their horse to take on the ride. Nate mounted his horse and watched as George mounted his. He didn't seem overly confident in the saddle but held his own.

Once the group started across the field, Nate caught up to Ockham. "I just remembered I have an important correspondence I must pen immediately. I shall catch up to the group as soon as I can."

"I understand," Ockham replied. "Will you be able to find your way?"

"Certainly. I'll see if someone wants to return with me so I'm not wandering around alone in search of the group."

Ockham nodded. "Very well. We are making our way to the pond. We shall see you soon."

Nate turned around and rode up beside George, who eyed him curiously.

"I must get a missive out straight away. Would you be willing to return with me and then we shall catch up to the group?" Nate needed to ensure that if anyone was listening, they heard the same story he had given Ockham.

"Of course, my lord," George responded, thankfully not asking any questions.

Once George turned around, they rode alongside each other.

"What are you doing?" George asked once they were out of earshot.

"Orchestrating a way for us to be alone. Just follow my lead."

They arrived back at the stables and Nate climbed down and handed his reins to the groom. "Lord Knox is going to wait for me here while I pen a missive, and then we shall rejoin the party."

The groom nodded, and Nate made his way back to his chamber. He picked up the satchel he had packed earlier and penned a quick missive to his estate manager to check in on things there. It wasn't an urgent missive, but no one else needed to know that. At least if anyone should ask, he penned a missive and sent it out.

Nate departed his room with the satchel and the sealed missive. He found a footman and asked them to ensure it was posted right away, then made his way back to the stables.

"Thank you for agreeing to wait for me, my lord. I would hate to lose my way on my own," Nate said, only for the groom's benefit.

"It was no trouble, my lord. Did you tend to your missive?"

"Indeed. We can be off now."

Nate climbed back atop his horse, and they trotted beside each other. They continued in the direction the group had departed until they were out of sight of the stables, just in case the groom paid attention to where they went.

"So this was your plan?" George asked, amused.

"There is surely a folly or cabin somewhere out here." Nate suddenly came to a stop, looking at George, who also quickly stopped. "I expect nothing from you. You know that, right? If you only wish to talk and enjoy a few quiet moments without others around, that would be enough for me."

George laughed. "If you don't find us somewhere soon, I shall make you strip right here."

Nate bit his bottom lip, his growing bulge becoming more uncomfortable in the saddle. "Very well, then. Let's go this way."

They started their horses through a grouping of trees and crossed a clearing. They were going in the direction opposite of where the party had gone, which should work in their favor. In a quarter hour, they came across a little cabin, which appeared to be used for hunting.

"Wait here," Nate said, climbing down from his horse.

He peeked in the windows, and there was no one inside. At least if they encountered anyone, he could say they were lost trying to find their group.

He tried the door, and it was unlocked. The cabin had only two rooms. One room had a settee and chairs before a fireplace and the other room was a bedchamber with a bed, dresser, and fireplace. It appeared as if it had gone unused for a long time, which would suit their needs just fine.

Nate went back to the open door and waved to George. "Get your handsome arse in here," he called out to him, enjoying the privacy they had alone in the woods.

He watched George climb down from his horse. George secured the reins of both horses and joined Nate in the doorway.

Nate grabbed his hand and pulled him inside, closing the door before pushing George up against it. He tossed his own hat onto the settee, then plucked George's hat off his head and did the same. "What do you think?" Nate asked, then placed a stream of kisses along George's jaw until he reached his ear, taking the lobe between his teeth. He loved the way George responded to him, pressing his bulge against Nate's.

"It's perfect," George replied, wrapping his arms around Nate's neck, releasing a soft whimper when Nate dipped his tongue into his ear. "Only because you are here."

"Tell me what you wish to do," Nate said, tugging at George's cravat, so he could obtain access to his neck. Nate quickly removed his gloves so he could feel George's skin beneath his bare fingers.

"First," George started. "I want your clothes off your body. I am dying to see what you look like."

Nate sucked and licked George's neck and collarbone. "Are you going to help me?"

George removed his gloves, dropped them on the floor, then began working the buttons of Nate's coat and pushed it off his shoulders. He set it over the back of a chair. They would have to help each other redress later to ensure they were presentable to join the group.

Nate did the same for George, quickly removing his coat and waistcoat. Their hands moved in a frenzy of unbuttoning clothing as George got Nate's waistcoat off and they worked on each other's shirts. Clothing stacked up on the back of the chair, in a matter of moments, they were both bare-chested, naked from the waist up before each other.

George placed his palms on Nate's chest and ran his fingers through the smattering of hair across the taut muscles. Nate's breath caught and he reveled in the way George's hands explored his body. Nate gave him time to explore, letting him touch every inch of his torso, watching as George licked his lips—the action caused his cock to throb.

Nate ran his hands down George's broad shoulders, down his smooth back until he clasped George's clothed bottom and pulled him against his body. "Remove your breeches."

Nate released him, and George worked to kick off his boots and socks. Nate did the same, not wishing to delay what they both wanted any longer. George stood before him in only his breeches, the only clothing keeping him from fully seeing him bared before him.

George caught Nate's gaze and began unfastening the buttons, then pushed the fabric over his hips, letting them fall to the floor.

"You are so completely perfect," Nate said, stepping closer so he could take George's cock in his hand. He stroked it a few times before removing his hand to un-button his own breeches. He stepped out of them when they hit the floor, grabbed George's hand, and pulled him with him.

Nate picked up the satchel and led George to the bedchamber.

Once they were in the room, he kicked the door closed with his foot and walked George backwards until his bottom touched the bed.

"You must tell me what you want," Nate said. "I don't want to do anything you aren't ready for."

George wrapped his arms around Nate's neck and brought their lips together. He dipped his tongue inside Nate's mouth, and it tasted like heaven and a spot of tea. He would never tire of tasting the man.

George shifted his kisses to Nate's neck and chest. "I want you inside of me."

"Inside of you where?" Nate asked, needing him to be clear about what he wanted. "I will be happy being with you in any way you are comfortable. I just want this to be everything you want it to be. We have our lives to explore each other."

George sucked and licked the hardened nipples on Nate's chest. "I want your cock in my arse."

Nate released a low growl. "Are you certain? It will hurt a bit, but I'll do my best to prevent as much pain as possible."

George stopped what he was doing and captured Nate's gaze. "I have never been more certain. This is what I want. *You* are what I want."

Nate gripped George's bottom and lifted him to sit on the bed. He kissed him hard for several moments before breaking the kiss. "Lie back on the bed," Nate instructed.

He grabbed the satchel and pulled out a jar of oil he had packed and set it within reach on the bed. He hadn't been certain if they would need it but decided it would be best to come prepared.

Nate looked down and took in the sight before him. The man who worked his way into Nate's heart more and more every moment lay across the bed with his firm body and his erect cock waiting for him. It was the most tantalizing sight he had ever seen. He lowered his head and took George's cock all the way to the base in one movement, sucking and licking as he worked his mouth up slowly until he reached the head. He placed a light kiss on the tip and then flicked it with his tongue.

George moaned and gripped the blanket beneath him.

Nate spread George's legs further and ran his tongue along the tight, puckered hole of his arse. The action alone might have made him spend. He pushed the tip of his tongue inside, stretching the hole wider.

"Fuck," George moaned, causing Nate to grin at the reaction he had already pulled from him. He had barely begun.

Nate licked and teased a few moments longer before lifting his head and taking the jar in his hands. "Do you wish for me to continue?" Nate asked, mostly teasing, since he was pretty sure he knew the answer.

"God, yes," George replied.

Nate removed the lid and dipped a finger inside, coating it in the oil. He rubbed the oil around the tight hole, which was about to be stretched as it never had before. Nate pressed the tip of his finger inside, shifting it deeper slowly, knuckle by knuckle, allowing George to adjust to him. He withdrew his finger and slid it all the way back inside in a single, fluid movement, reveling in George's ragged breathing. Nate continued in that way, his own cock throbbing in response to George's moaning and panting.

He withdrew his finger and dipped two fingers into the oil that time, then inserted them both with the same slow care he gave the first time. Once he allowed George to adjust, he worked his fingers in and out. Nate ached with each movement of his hand, imagining what his cock was going to feel like in place of his fingers.

He hooked his fingers and put added pressure on the area he knew would bring George even more pleasure, and he was rewarded with a steady stream of moans and profanities. He twisted his fingers, opening and stretching George's arse as much as he could.

"I'm going to use my cock now," Nate said, removing his fingers.

"Yes. Please, Nate," George pleaded.

Nate loved how much George wanted him and that he was the one introducing him to the pleasure they would share together.

He dipped his fingers in the oil again and rubbed a line of it along George's cock. "Stroke yourself," he said.

George did as instructed and worked the oil around his shaft.

"That's really good," he groaned.

Nate covered his fingers again and applied it to himself that time, giving his length a few quick strokes as he coated his shaft, realizing just how little it would take for him to spend.

Nate put the lid back on the jar and set it aside. He hooked his arms under George's bent knees and pulled him closer so his arse hung just over the edge of the bed. He positioned himself at George's opening, teasing it with the head of his cock, which he was certain was driving himself madder than it was George.

He pushed the head of his cock inside, pausing to allow George to adjust to him. He moved another inch and paused again. Nate continued with the agonizing slowness until he was ballocks deep.

"Are you alright?" Nate asked when George's hand stopped stroking his cock.

"Yes." George sighed. "I don't want to spend yet."

Nate licked his lips and moved inside of George's arse. He pulled out and pushed himself back in. He did so again, forcing himself to make slow, controlled movements.

"Harder, Nate," George cried out. "I'm not going to break."

Unable to control himself any longer, Nate thrust himself hard against George's arse. He withdrew and thrust with quick, hard strokes, pounding into him. George began stroking himself again. "Fuck, that is so good," George ground out. "Don't fucking stop."

Nate turned feral from George's command and thrust with such intensity, gripping George's thighs so hard, he might leave a mark. Nothing had ever felt so good or as intense as it did with George. He longed to fill George with his seed, possessing the man as his own.

After a few more hard thrusts, George moaned Nate's name when he spent, covering his toned stomach with the proof of his climax. Nate shoved himself as deep as he could, spending deep inside George's arse, moving in small pulsations to extend his climax and work every drop of the warm liquid from his body.

Nate withdrew slowly, trying to catch his breath. It had been the most vivid, powerful climax he had ever had, and it had knocked him off his axis. Everything about George had him thinking and feeling things he never thought he'd feel again, let alone with such intensity.

Fighting to get his thoughts and vision back, he reached into the satchel again and pulled out a couple of cloths he had packed. He wiped George's stomach clean, glancing up to find George propping his hands behind his head to watch him.

Wiping away his seed that had leaked from George's arse, he already couldn't wait until he could take him again. After tossing the cloths on top of the satchel, he helped George shift further onto the bed and climbed in beside him, both of them lying across the bed with their feet hanging off the side.

Nate wrapped his arms around George and held him close.

"I had no idea," George whispered. "I never even imagined."

"Does that mean you are satisfied?"

"Quite. I am going to need you again soon."

Nate laughed. "Not too soon, handsome. You are going to be sore. You might have to settle for me sucking your cock for a day or two."

George pretended to pout. "I suppose that shall suffice."

"Although you might hate me when you have to get back in the saddle."

George placed a sweet kiss on his lips. "It shall be my reminder that I am yours and you are mine."

Nate's heart raced at George's words.

"If I do my job right, you shouldn't need so many reminders," Nate said, kissing George's brow, pressing his cheek against it as he held him tighter.

"I hope it's always like this," George said, his words almost a sigh.

Nate grinned. "I hope so, too." He would do everything in his power to make it so.

"What happens when we leave at the end of the house party?"

Nate sighed and urged George to get up from the bed, even though he'd have lain there with him for days if he could have. "That is a conversation for later as we must rejoin the group," Nate replied. "We have been gone far too long. We shall have to pretend we got ourselves lost and hope we don't accidentally do that very thing."

Chapter 6

George had to admit that getting back atop a horse was a bit more uncomfortable after the state of ecstasy Nate put him in, but it was well worth it. He may even be a changed man after that experience. He was certainly even deeper in love with Nate, and he hoped they might discuss how things would work between them in the future. They couldn't live together. Society would never accept such a thing.

The voice of his father crept back into his head, and he fought to push it away. His father would likely take a whip to him if he knew of what George had done and who he was certain that he loved. He thought about what his relationship, or whatever they might call it, with Nate would mean for his estate and his tenants. He still had others who depended on him.

He also wasn't certain how he could ever be expected to sire an heir. Although he had always thought it would be nice to have children. He would never betray his love for Nate by lying with anyone else, man or woman. Even if Nate were understanding and agreed to some sort of arrangement, George was unlikely to find the ability to perform the necessary acts. His heart hurt thinking about Nate being in the same predicament. He had a title he may wish to pass on, and he would be able to bed a woman. What if the woman should fall in love with him? George didn't care for the notion, but it was among the matters they must discuss.

"Something troubling you? Are you in any pain?" Nate asked quietly from atop his horse, trotting beside George.

George looked around to see how close the others in the group were to them. They had found the group and slipped in to join the party for the picnic. They each sat on different blankets, acting as if they hadn't just rejoined the group together. George sought Lady Lily, believing that was what he would be expected to do to keep up appearances. The pretense of it all was draining.

After the picnic, they all started the journey back, hoping to beat the rain. Lord Callan had accompanied

Lady Lily, so Nate and George had trailed behind some of the others.

"Just thinking," George replied. "And only a little."

"What is on your mind?" Nate asked, apparently unwilling to let the matter drop.

"We can't discuss it here."

Nate nodded in understanding. "Very well. Tonight, then."

George said nothing in response, not wishing to draw too much attention to the time they were spending in each other's company.

There was a crack of lightning and then a loud rumble of thunder. George looked up at the sky as a few raindrops hit his face. "We need to go faster," he called to Nate.

They took their horses to a gallop, more raindrops hitting George's face. They continued as fast as they could. The others in the party followed suit, all racing for the stables. After racing across the fields, the sky erupted and doused them in buckets of rain just as they reached the waiting groom.

It was enough to soak them, even though they had only been in it for a few moments. George leapt from his horse and tossed the reins to the groom, hurrying towards the house. He knew Nate wasn't far behind him. They hurried in behind the group of ladies from the riding party.

Once they were inside the house, the ladies hurried off, likely to seek dry clothes. George looked at Nate, loving the way his face was flushed from the exertion and chilly rain. George bit his bottom lip and quickly got control of himself, remembering they weren't alone.

"I am going to retire to my chamber for a while. I should need to change," George said, speaking to Nate as if they were nothing but acquaintances.

"I believe I am in need of the same," Nate replied, matching George's indifference.

It slightly concerned George that Nate could school his features so easily, but it was vital to their continued acceptance in society.

They fell in step beside each other, ascending the stairs and then traversing the hall to their respective chambers. Once George reached his door, Nate kept walking but brushed his fingers against George's as he passed, not looking back.

George entered his chamber and locked it. He wasn't ready to ring for his valet just yet. A fire had been set in the fireplace, which he appreciated. He moved closer to it and warmed himself. He removed his gloves and hat, tossed them in the chair, and stripped off the rest of his clothing.

He recalled the events of earlier and it aided in warming him. He imagined Nate just next door, stripping the wet clothes from his body and standing before his own fire. So close, yet also so far away.

That is what their life would consist of if they wished to be together. Both of them could hang if anyone were to discover what they were to each other.

Releasing a sad sigh, George ran his hand down his face. They should be able to be together when they wished.

But George heard his father's voice in his head, reminding him of all his duties. If George's father were alive, he might string George up himself for the risk to the title and the family name.

George wasn't certain how long he could stomach the sneaking around that would be required to only have stolen moments together. But he also didn't believe he could give Nate up. So what else could they do?

After dinner that evening, the gentlemen only remained behind for a quarter hour, since the ladies of the house party would perform a round of musical entertainment for them. George had always enjoyed music and looked forward to hearing the talent of the women in attendance.

He leaned against one windowsill with a fresh tumbler of brandy and listened to the first performance. The young lady was quite talented.

Lady Eliza and Lady Juliet then performed a duet, playing and singing together. They were the highlight of the evening, earning them the loudest applause. George thought to motion for Nate to meet him on the terrace again, but he noticed Lord Irvine was escorting Lady Eliza to that very location.

There were a few more performances, all enjoyable to listen to. Afterwards, the guests began forming groups of conversation around the room.

George glanced at Nate and found that the man was walking in his direction. Nate nodded to him with perfect aristocratic indifference. "Excellent performances, were they not?" he said.

"Indeed, my lord." George fought his annoyance at the way Nate must play the role of the stuffy marquess when they were among others.

Nate brought his drink to his lips. "Come to my chamber tonight."

"Isn't that a bit risky?" George asked, also taking a sip and looking around the room, pretending he was looking for Lady Lily.

"The ground is far too wet to go outside. I'll knock on the wall when my valet has left. Then come when you are sure the hallway is clear."

George nodded. "Very well."

Nate gave him a polite nod and moved on to join a conversation with Lady Juliet and Lord Camden.

He was unsure why everything seemed to annoy him that evening. George had the best afternoon of his life with the man he believed he had fallen in love with. If they lived in a different society, perhaps the notion wouldn't be so scandalous. Perhaps that was the source of his irritation. Whatever it was, he was in a foul mood and didn't feel much like making small talk with any of the other guests.

George refilled his glass with a healthy pour of brandy and took it with him as he retired to his chamber. He was better off being irritated on his own, in the bit of privacy that was afforded to him.

Tanner, his valet, knocked on the door, and George admitted him. George removed his clothing and donned his banyan, as he typically slept nude. He dismissed Tanner for the evening, and groaned when he realized he would have to dress again to sneak into Nate's chamber. It was risky enough already, but doing so donning a banyan wrapped around his naked form would be much harder to explain if he were caught.

George dropped himself onto his settee and picked up his drink. He'd await the knock and then he'd slip on a shirt and breeches. He stared into the fire, slowly sipping his brandy until it was gone. George imagined himself in Nate's arms, an act that would certainly aid in improving his mood.

A half an hour passed, and George became concerned he might have missed the knock. Although he wasn't certain when Nate would retire for the evening, given that George had disappeared early.

He closed his eyes for what seemed like only a few moments, imagining what it might be like to have the acceptance to introduce Nate to the world as his partner, his lover, perhaps even his husband.

George woke up to warm lips pressed against his. He blinked his eyes open. "I didn't mean to startle you, but I just had to kiss you," Nate said, leaning over him.

"Shite, I must have drifted off, waiting for the knock. I'm sorry. What time is it?"

"About that," Nate started, "I don't know how I failed to notice that there is a door between our chambers. We must be in a set of rooms that can be used as a suite."

George sat up and looked over Nate's shoulder, seeing into the other chamber.

"Well, that is certainly more convenient," George said.

"I locked your chamber door, and mine, of course." Nate held his hand out to George and pulled him to stand when George clasped it.

George noticed that Nate only donned a banyan as well. He ran his hands beneath it and found Nate's bare chest. He pushed the banyan off his shoulders and let it fall to the floor. Nate did the same to him, so they stood naked before each other. Nate pulled back the covers. "Get into bed, handsome."

George did as he said and watched as Nate stepped away to blow out all the candles in the room, leaving them with only the moonlight and the light cast from the flames in the fireplace. He stoked the fire and added another log. The view of Nate's naked backside flexing while he worked caused George's breath to catch.

Once Nate had tended to the fire, he joined George in the bed and pulled the covers over them. "At least we shall be able to share a bed all night without fear of not waking up early enough to return to our correct chambers."

"We should be able to sleep wherever we damn well please," George ground out.

"Is that what has you in such a state?" Nate asked, wrapping his arms around George.

George rested his head on Nate's chest and wrapped his arm around his waist.

"Doesn't it bother you? We are grown men who should be free to do as we please."

Nate sighed. "Of course it does. It certainly gives one perspective on the challenges that women face. If they should marry the wrong man, they are considered among the same standing as property and cattle."

"Do you intend to marry?" George asked, realizing he asked the question with a more irritated edge to his tone than he intended.

"I don't know. I thought I might marry once, but she thankfully found her true love. I'd much prefer for her to do so. Everyone deserves that chance."

George glanced up at him. "Were you attracted to her?"

"No, nothing like that. She would have kept my secrets, and I would have enabled her freedom. I'll introduce you to her soon. She'd love to meet you."

"But would you have given her children?" George didn't know why he couldn't let it go, but he wanted to understand.

Nate shrugged. "Probably so, since we both wanted them, but what does it matter? She actually informed me she's with child in her most recent letter."

When he didn't say anything in response, Nate gripped his chin and lifted it to look at him.

"Being able to 'perform' the necessities to create a babe doesn't mean I will want a woman, George. I'm not attracted to every man who crosses my path, either, as I am sure it is the same for you." Nate drew a deep breath and stared into George's eyes with such affection that George's heart leapt into his throat.

"I know it's fast, but I love you, George. *You.* And I only want you. These decisions about our future are ones we shall make together, if you wish for us to have a future."

George pressed his lips to Nate's. "I love you, too," George whispered, still in disbelief that the man beside him loved him the same George did. "Of course I want a future with you. Nothing about our future is simple."

"I am glad you are asking me questions and talking to me about your concerns. I don't want you worried about anything regarding what I feel for you. I will reassure you every minute of every day for as long as you need."

George nodded against Nate's chest. He wasn't certain he'd ever feel confident that the rug wouldn't get pulled out from under them at any moment, but at least at that moment, he was safe and in the arms of the man he loved, and he'd savor it for as long as he could.

Nate ran his hand along George's back until he gripped the cheek of his arse, giving it a gentle squeeze. Their legs tangled together and George's cock hardened and he pressed himself tighter against Nate so their cocks rubbed against each other.

"I seem to recall you saying something about sucking my cock earlier," George said, placing a few kisses along Nate's chest.

Nate slid down further on the bed. "Place your knees on either side of my head and face the footboard."

George looked up at him, confused at his direction, and then he realized what that position would enable them to do. He kissed Nate, licking along his lips and suckling his tongue before he came up onto his knees and did as Nate instructed.

Guiding his cock into Nate's open mouth, George then lay across Nate's body. He sucked Nate's length into his mouth, enjoying the intensity of giving and receiving such pleasure at the same time. In the position George was in, he moved his hips to move himself deeper into Nate's mouth, then sucked Nate's cock with the same intensity. Nate bucked beneath him, thrusting upward to match George's thrusts, both fucking each other's mouths with increased speed.

Gripping the cheeks of Nate's arse, George spread them further while he continued sucking and ran his finger along the puckered hole. Nate moaned around George's cock, and George pressed the tip of his finger just inside the tight hole.

When George tasted the salty heat of Nate's release, he stilled his hips as he also spent, rocking slowly into Nate's mouth until his lengthy orgasm subsided.

George was too tired to move for a moment and drew several deep breaths to return his breathing to normal. Nate finally urged him to shift and return to his side, cradling George in his arms again.

"You need sleep, handsome," Nate said. "You hardly slept last night, and you exerted yourself in more ways than one today. I'll be right here when you wake, and I have a plan that shall see us spend most of the day in bed together tomorrow."

"What is this plan?" George asked, slightly amused.

"I'll explain it in the morning. For now, close your eyes."

Nate lazily ran his hand along George's back, and it was quite effective at lulling him into a state of intense relaxation. He nestled in against Nate, and that was the last thing he remembered before he drifted off to sleep.

Chapter 7

There was nothing better than waking up with George in his arms. It wasn't a luxury that they might be afforded regularly, depending on where they each needed to be, so Nate would revel in it as long as he could. George wasn't wrong to be frustrated that they had to be so careful in how and when they expressed their love for each other.

Nate stared at George's head resting on his chest, wishing he never had to move from where they lay. He had never thought he'd find love the first time, much less a second time. He held him tighter. After the devastation of such a loss the first time, his heart wouldn't survive if something were to happen to George.

George stirred and shifted his chin up to meet his gaze. "Good morning," he said, his eyes only half open.

"I must return to my chamber before either of our valets should knock."

"I don't want you to go."

Nate groaned at the realization that George's cock was hard and resting on his thigh.

"I told you, I have a plan."

"I'm listening," George said, running his fingers through the hair on Nate's chest.

Nate's cockstand made a tent out of the blanket, and it was going to be agony until he could return.

"You are going to tell your valet you don't feel well and wish to rest today. Say it was the cold from the rain. Let him bring you a tray and fuss over you while I go down to breakfast."

Confusion marred George's face. "I don't understand."

"Well, after breakfast, I'll make a show of having a megrim, thus needing to return to my chamber. At least if one of us dresses and goes downstairs, it would appear less suspicious. We shall each tell our valets we wish to rest and will ring when we have need of them. Then you are all mine." Nate pressed his lips to George's, not deepening the kiss, else he wouldn't be able to remove himself from George's bed.

When Nate pulled back, George began placing soft kisses on his chest, pulling a low groan from Nate. "You must stop, or I shan't leave."

"You had better go then," George said, giving him the most tempting look.

Nate tossed the covers off himself and climbed out of the bed, turning to spread the blankets back over George. He grabbed his banyan and wrapped it around himself.

"I'm going to unlock your door so you don't have to get out of bed when you ring for your valet."

George nodded, and Nate crossed the room back to him and placed one more kiss on his lips. "I shall return as soon as I can."

"See that you do," George playfully returned.

After unlocking the door to George's chamber, Nate quickly returned to his own room through the adjoining door and locked it behind him. He unlocked his own chamber door and rang for his valet. The sooner he got dressed and broke his fast, the sooner he could return.

Thompson arrived a few moments later. While Thompson shaved him, he hoped George forwent his own shave that morning. He had to push the thought aside, or his valet would surely be scandalized by his reaction. After his shave, Nate dressed and begrudgingly went downstairs to get it over with. At least he'd get to eat something, since he wasn't certain when they would emerge from their chambers again.

At breakfast, Nate noted that Viscount Callan was seated with Lady Lily. He couldn't hear the conversation that the two were having, but something about the way they glanced at each other made Nate pay closer attention. When they each thought the other wasn't looking, he noted something in their expressions, which indicated there was affection between them, even if they weren't ready to admit it to each other, or themselves, yet. Good for them.

At least Lady Lily wouldn't be devastated when George decided not to offer for her after all. With that matter settled, he supposed he and George could discuss what each of their plans might be when they left the house party. It wasn't as if Nate could move George into his home, or vice versa, as much as he wished that were the case.

Nate ensured he sat near his hosts during breakfast. He needed them to hear his request, hoping that it would aid the notion that he wasn't feeling his best. When most of the guests had arrived, he flagged a footman down and asked his valet to be summoned to bring up a tisane to his chamber.

"Are you not feeling well, Lord Demming?" Lady Ockham asked.

"Just a bit of a megrim. I am certain that a bit more rest will be just the thing."

"Be sure to ring if you need anything," she replied. "Lord Knox isn't feeling well this morning, either."

Nate feigned indifference at her comment and rubbed his temple for good measure. He didn't enjoy lying and sneaking around, but it was necessary until such a day that society might see matters of love differently. It was either walk away from George and a chance of happiness, or give into the need for the occasional ruse. He would always choose the latter.

"If you will excuse me, I shall return to my chamber. I hope to rejoin the group soon." Another lie.

Once Nate reached the stairs, he grinned to himself. All he had to do was wait for Thompson to bring up the tisane, and then he could return to George. He entered his room and removed the clothing he had just donned. He slipped his banyan back around himself and tied it closed.

He sat in one of the chairs in his chamber, rapping his fingers on the armrest, waiting for Thompson to knock at the door. Minutes felt like hours, but the knock finally came.

"Enter."

Thompson approached with a cup. "Here you are, my lord."

"Thank you. I am going to rest for a while and will ring for you when I feel like rejoining the party."

Thompson gave him a quick bow and departed the room.

Nate quickly rose from his chair and crossed the room to lock the door. Finally. He set the cup down by the washbasin and made his way to the door that led to George. He unlocked it and opened the door, which pushed out into George's room.

He poked his head into the room and came almost face to face with a man. Hell and damnation. The man assessed him, and Nate did his best to hide himself behind the door so the man might not notice that Nate had bare feet and only wore a banyan.

"I just wished to see if Lord Knox was all right as I heard he wasn't feeling well from our hosts. I find I am suffering a megrim and thought perhaps there could be some sort of ailment going around." Nate assumed the man was George's valet based on his clothing and hoped he wouldn't examine the story too closely. It really didn't explain why a marquess would attempt to enter in Nate's current state of dress, or lack thereof.

"He is resting, my lord."

"Well, give him my best."

Nate closed the door and locked it, not giving the man a chance to respond and hoping he heard the lock and assumed that would be the last of Nate entering his lordship's chamber.

He paced his chamber, hoping George's valet wasn't a man prone to gossip. He also knew he couldn't risk entering again without some kind of signal from George. If the man was still in there, there would be no acceptable excuse.

Nate waited for a quarter hour, continuing his constant pacing and hoping for a knock from George. After another half an hour, he worried he should do some kind of damage control. If he rejoined the party, perhaps that would dissuade any talk if there should be any. At least if he were downstairs mingling with guests and perhaps flirting with a few of the ladies, ones whom he knew wouldn't favor him, no one could accuse him of having a tryst with a man upstairs.

A sigh escaped Nate's lips. He should have considered that George's valet could have been present. It was a foolish mistake and one that could cost them if he didn't act quickly.

He reached for the bellpull to ring for Thompson. There was nothing else he could do. He had to do his best to ensure that even if the valet should say something, the rest of the house party would believe otherwise.

Thompson knocked, and Nate unlocked the door.

"I am ready to dress again. I am feeling much more the thing after a bit of rest."

He dressed in the items Thompson sat out for him and let his valet help him back into his coats. Once dressed again, he departed from his chamber. When he passed by George's door. His heart pained, longing to barge into his room. To hell with what anyone would have to say about it.

But he kept walking and when he arrived downstairs, he found that there was a group trip planned to visit the village. He groaned to himself. Not only were their plans for the day ruined, but he'd have to attend the trip and leave George behind at the house. He cursed under his breath since he only had himself to blame for attempting such a risky rendezvous.

Nate gathered with the other guests, joining Lady Preston and St. Albans as they all waited for a coach. Plastering his best polite smile on his face, he did his best not to look as irritated as he felt. It was going to be a very long day, indeed.

Chapter 8

George was worried and almost in a state of panic after Tanner saw Nate attempting to enter the chamber. Part of him wanted to be angry at Nate over the situation, but then he felt guilty. He knew Nate hadn't intended for Tanner to see him, but shouldn't he have considered that George might not be alone? If he had only arrived five minutes later, the whole thing would have been avoided. Tanner had only returned to clear the breakfast trays.

The whole thing was madness. Tanner wasn't prone to gossip, but he couldn't be certain whether the man left the room with or without a bit of suspicion. He had certainly never encountered George in a compromising situation with a woman, but hopefully, the man would soon forget all about it. But if Tanner suspected anything, it put Nate and George at greater risk. If he were to encounter them together in such a way again, he was sure to suspect the truth. That couldn't happen.

George debated knocking on the wall to let Nate know when Tanner left, but he was still a bit shaken by the whole turn of events. Perhaps they had been taking too many risks, and it was a sign that they needed to take more care. So he opted not to do so. He didn't think Nate would take the risk again, at least not until much later.

If Nate didn't reappear after a while, George decided he would dress and rejoin the other guests. He didn't wish to sit in his chamber by himself all day. He would just need to wait long enough that his hosts would believe that it was plausible that he was feeling better. Grabbing his book from the bedside table, he did his best to focus on reading instead of all the rumors and gossip that could possibly be starting about them already.

He chastised himself for jumping to such conclusions and letting his imagination run away from him. Tanner had always been a loyal servant, and he had no reason to believe that even if the man found the situation to be odd that he would say anything about it.

George shook off his concerns and refocused his attention on his book, forcing himself to read the words aloud to help him focus. That seemed to do the trick as before long, he was caught up in the story. After a few chapters, he glanced at the clock, and it had been almost two hours since he last checked.

He stretched and decided he should dress and make an appearance downstairs. George reached for the bellpull to have Tanner attend him again.

He tried to push thoughts of Nate away as Tanner shaved him and then helped him to dress. George wished he knew if Nate was even still in his chamber. He would know soon enough when he joined the other guests. They wouldn't be able to speak to each other, at least not at first, as they would need to keep their distance.

George ventured downstairs and didn't see anyone else at first. There wasn't a roar of voices or the sound of any games being played. He continued through the foyer and there were a couple of gentlemen chatting near a window in the salon, Lord Irvine and Lord Percy.

Based on the reputations of each of the gentlemen, they weren't the sort that George usually spent much time with, but he could start there and hope he might determine where the rest of the guests were. He longed to at least catch a glimpse of Nate, even if he couldn't speak to him.

"Gentlemen," George said, approaching them.

"Knox," Irvine said. "Good to see you are well."

For a moment, George almost didn't understand what the man meant but caught himself. "Yes, indeed. Just needed a bit of rest." George made a show of glancing around the room. "Where is everyone? This is still a house party, is it not?"

Percy laughed. "Most of the others are on a shopping trip to the village. Irvine here is still nursing his pride, so I took pity on him."

Irvine scowled at the man. "I am doing no such thing."

George eyed them curiously. "What happened?"

"Irvine actually thought he had a chance to bed that Lady Eliza chit, but she left to marry Craven."

Irvine shrugged. "It's of little importance to me. I don't have a shortage of willing bed warmers. But a taste of her cunt would certainly have been appealing. Not a man here could deny that. Am I right, Knox?"

"Indeed," George replied with as much enthusiasm as he could muster. He had grown accustomed to such pretense, but it irked more than it used to, and it wasn't overly palatable before either.

Percy jumped in. "Did you see the chest on Lady Juliet? Damn. And Duncan is working hard to get her down the aisle so he can bury his face in those. The fool."

George fought rolling his eyes and forced himself to pretend he cared about their taxing conversation. Surely there was anyone else still in the house he could speak with. If he wished hard enough, perhaps someone else would appear.

"What about Lady Lily, Knox? Are you still thinking of offering for her? Given that she's a bluestocking, I'm not sure how exciting she would be," Irvine asked.

"We'll see how the rest of the house party goes. But I think she has a lot more to her than others realize," George replied, his tone hinting as something that he had no idea whether it was true. He hated himself for even saying it. He only hoped his words wouldn't have either of these men sniffing around the poor lady's skirts.

Percy laughed. "Are you telling us you've already tried her out a bit, Knox? I mean, that is one of the benefits of a house party."

"Not yet, but we still have many days left," George said, faking a smirk. He hoped that if they believed him to be interested in such things, they'd at least leave the lady alone.

"I'm just glad there aren't any Mollys at this house party," Irvine said, his words causing George's throat to go dry. "I heard there was another Molly house near Fleet Street. Nothing but disgusting filth."

George used every ounce of control to school his features and hope he didn't give any clue to his discomfort.

"What do you care where a man wants to stick his prick? As long as we don't have to see it," Percy said, laughing and waving the man off.

"Because it's not right and not natural. And what if those fops should look at us and get ideas?" Irvine asked, the disdain and hatred clear in his tone.

George continued to watch and listen, doing his best to hide his anger, or worse, to allow tears to form.

"None of the Mollys are looking at you, Irvine," Percy said, smacking his back. "You can't seal the deal with a lady, so perhaps you might change your tune when desperation sets in."

Irvine clenched his fists. "There is a reason it's illegal and a hanging offense. Such things have no place in polite society. And let's sneak out to the pub tonight and you can watch how fast I have a woman bouncing on my cock."

His words made George think about himself, or worse, Nate, suffering such a fate. He could never allow such a thing to happen. There may be a few people who would accept them, but the opinion and beliefs of Irvine were common across most of their society. Not to mention their love was against the law.

It would break his heart to walk away from Nate, but better that than watching him hang. His heart splintered, pushing aside any romantic ideals that might trick him into thinking that any kind of life together was feasible. It wasn't. They were fooling themselves. If Nate couldn't see it, George would be the strong one.

"What about you, Knox? Want to join us tonight and place bets on whether Irvine here can seal the deal with some big-breasted barmaid?" Percy asked.

He forced a laugh, swallowing down all his heartbreak. None of it would serve him. "I think I might see about Lady Lily instead." He didn't mean it the way it sounded, or how they would interpret it, but it was of no matter to him. If they thought he was going to bed the lady, all the better.

"Best of luck there," Percy replied. "I hope she's got a wicked mouth on her."

If George thought he could fight well enough to take both of the men on his own, he would. He could take them one on one, but both would pose greater difficulty. They deserved to be knocked to the ground for their horrid, vile words. They were the epitome of what was wrong with society. Their behavior was tolerated and encouraged in some circles, while love was limited to how men of similar ideals defined it.

What was the use of fighting it? There was no other choice. He'd have to marry a woman and do what was expected of him, and that was that. And he'd never see Nate again once he ended things.

Before any further improper talk could come from either of the two bounders, some of the other guests entered the parlor. The group returned from the village, and George knew the moment that Nate entered the salon, as he felt his presence before he saw him. He fought to keep his breathing under control and refused to look at him.

George removed himself from any further conversation with Lords Percy and Irvine and sought out a different circle to converse with. A half an hour had passed as he mostly remained quiet and listened to others speak, doing his best to avoid looking at Nate.

Seeing him from the corner of his eye, he focused his gaze away from him, when he finally saw Lady Lily entering from the terrace.

Resolved in what his future held. The way it had always been meant to be and what he had planned for his life before he had even known of Nate's existence. He drew a fortifying breath and crossed the room to her.

He went to her and clasped her hand in his, then brought her knuckles to his lips. "I hope you will forgive me for failing to escort you today, my lady. I would have enjoyed such an honor."

With each word he spoke, he lost pieces of his heart and soul that he knew he'd never get back, and there wasn't a damn thing anyone could do about it.

Chapter 9

Nate didn't understand why George refused to look at him. At first, he thought he was imagining it, or that perhaps George just remained cautious after what had occurred. He hoped he wasn't angry at him for departing with the others on the village trip. He spent the entire time missing George and wondering what he did to entertain himself while most of the guests were gone.

By the time they had finished with dinner, George hadn't looked at him even once. And not from a lack of trying on Nate's part.

Once everyone returned from the village trip earlier that day, they had all gathered in the salon. Nate hoped to join in the same conversation George had found himself in, but he was speaking with a group of gentlemen. Once

Lady Lily had returned from a walk out to the terrace, George joined her and then never left her side.

Nate hadn't been able to tell him what he witnessed at breakfast and that he was almost positive the lady might have an interest in another man. George should leave her be and give her the chance to see if she might find a love match with Callan. And from everything Nate knew of the man, Callan was an upstanding gentleman.

Nate didn't want to interrupt a conversation with just the two of them without a good reason, so he chatted with other guests and waited for his opportunity.

Once tea was served, George settled on a settee with the lady. Afterward, he appeared to invite her for a walk in the gardens, since they disappeared for a while. Nate wasn't jealous exactly. He didn't believe that anything untoward would occur. It wasn't that. He just wished George might have at least acknowledged him somehow. Even just a quick smile or a passing glance. Something that told him all was well between them.

Was George mad at him for the incident with his valet? That was certainly possible, but he would hope that George knew he didn't intend for that to occur. And based on their interactions that day, he doubted anyone would think anything about it, even if his valet were to share the story.

Having had enough of trying to get George's attention, Nate thought of how to get him alone. He had to find a way to speak with him, even if only for a few moments.

Once everyone joined together in the salon after dinner, their hosts suggested a game of charades, which was the last thing Nate wished to do.

He couldn't concentrate on anything but George. Something was wrong. He knew in his heart that something was amiss. Something had changed between George and him, and he needed to know what it was.

The rest of the guests partook in the game, while Nate clenched his jaw and stared at George more often than he should have. George wasn't actively playing either, but Nate noticed that the man did a better job pretending than he had. In his mind, he pleaded for and willed George to look at him, even just once. If anyone were watching Nate, they would be sure to question why he kept staring at the earl. Not that he gave a fuck at that moment. The tiny bit of control he had to keep from shouting across the room to get George's attention was slipping through his fingers.

The game of charades ended, and George excused himself. Nate did the same, slipping out the other exit and moving as quickly as he could without drawing attention as he raced to catch up with George. He saw him ahead of him, almost to the stairs. Thankfully, there was no one else in sight. "George," he called out in a loud whisper.

George stopped in his tracks and turned on his heel to face him. Nate wasn't sure what he saw in his expression when George finally looked at him. Sadness, perhaps.

"We must speak," Nate said.

George looked around. "Not here."

"No, of course not. Will you knock on the wall when your valet has left?"

"Yes." George turned to walk away.

"George," Nate whispered again.

"Have a good evening, Lord Demming," George replied, glancing behind him and then turning on his heel and starting up the staircase.

The formality sounding from George's tongue almost made him cringe. He heard voices approaching from the hallway and understood why George would address him as such, but it felt far too formal after all they had shared. And all they meant to each other. Something about the tone in his voice gnawed at Nate, and he couldn't put his finger on it.

He forced himself to slowly climb the stairs and not chase after George. He would speak to him soon, and then all would be well.

Nate had dressed for bed, which meant he was naked besides covering himself with his banyan, and paced every inch of his chamber. He made himself turn and walk the same route in the alternate direction, if only to make his pacing feel somewhat different. After what felt like an eternity, a knock sounded on the wall. With no care about how foolish he looked, he took off running to the door, almost crashing into it while he worked the log and opened it into George's room.

"Love," Nate started, "I'm so sorry about earlier. I should have thought. I don't think we have anything to worry about."

George interrupted him, laughing. It wasn't a laugh that indicated he found what Nate had said funny, as there was a hard edge to it. Nate assessed him and noted he was wearing breeches with his banyan over them. Not exactly odd, but not what he expected, either.

"Nothing to worry about?" George stood from where he sat on the settee and waved his hand towards Nate. "You believe we have nothing to worry about? You don't think that continuing this"—he gestured between them—"will give us cause to have anything to worry about? Are you that dense?"

Nate flinched as if George had struck him, and at the way his entire body pained, he might as well have. "Why are you acting like this?"

"Because one of us has to. There isn't a future here and you know it."

Tears formed at the corners of Nate's eyes, and he urged himself to remain calm. "You don't mean that. We can figure it out."

"There is nothing to figure out. This is done. We are done."

"But we love each other, George. You can't ignore that."

George's jaw set and clenched, and he fisted his hands at his sides. "Are you willing to die for our love? Because that is the price."

Nate lost his battle, and the tears fell down his cheeks. He rushed to George and gripped his shoulders, forcing him to look at him. "Yes, dammit. Don't you see that? I would risk my life to love you."

George wrenched himself out of Nate's grasp. "And that's why we are done. I won't watch you hang. It's not romantic. It's foolish." George stepped behind the settee, putting a physical barrier between them. "I am going to marry Lady Lily."

Stepping behind the nearby chair, Nate needed something to steady himself. He wiped his face and allowed a few moments of silence to hang between them, while his mind raced through all the many things he'd like to say.

"You can't marry her," Nate finally said, the words barely above a whisper.

"You have no say in the matter. Marriage is what is expected of us."

Nate drew a long breath. "Are you going to be honest with her and tell her what kind of marriage she would have?"

"She will have the marriage many women of the *ton* desire. She will be provided for in a manner expected for a countess, and she can live her life as she wishes."

Nate fisted his hands, fighting to keep from throwing the chair before him across the room. "She may have an interest in Viscount Callan. Lady Lily deserves the truth. If she wants a marriage of love, she deserves that choice."

"That is more foolish nonsense, Lord Demming. Are you not paying attention? Titles and rules dictate our lives, not love."

"George," Nate ground out, but George raised his hand to stop him.

"Her father wants the match. I'm an earl and outrank Callan. The man will accept my suit for that reason alone. That's the way it's done. The sooner you select your wife and accept that fact, the sooner we will forget all about whatever this was."

Unable to control himself any longer, Nate rushed closer to George, causing him to back up against the wall where Nate pinned him and clasped his cheeks in his hands. "I love you, George." The tears steadily flowed down Nate's cheeks. If George would just look at him, he'd remember what they shared and that he didn't mean what he had said. He knew George loved him. He had to.

George looked for a moment as if he might change his mind on everything he said, and Nate allowed the hope to ease his aching heart. But only for a moment. Then George's expression hardened, and he pushed Nate back. "Yet the outcome is the same. Please depart from my chamber, Lord Demming."

Nate wanted to stay. He longed to hold him in his arms, kiss him and make George realize he was a fool for tossing away something as precious as what they shared for the benefit of the society. The members of that same society could be the ones to hang for all Nate cared. He'd move to the Americas or somewhere on the continent if that was what it took to be with George.

Fuck their titles and the rules that were forced upon them. But if George didn't believe in their love enough to fight for them and had already hardened towards him, he was fighting a losing battle. Could Nate love enough for both of them?

There wasn't a doubt in his mind that the voice of George's father had doused the fire that George might have once burned for Nate.

"Is this because of your father?" Nate asked. He knew it was. He knew from all they had shared that George still worried about what the man might think, even though he was dead and gone.

George's expression turned angry. "This is because it's the reality we live in. My father just happened to be right."

Nate shook his head and walked away to the open door between their chambers. He looked back at George, who had his back to him.

"I hope your father might finally be proud of you, Lord Knox."

Nate closed the door and locked it, not waiting to see if George would respond. He regretted the words right after he said them, knowing he only said them to hurt him. But if George wished to live for the expectations of a dead man, he was the foolish one.

Lying across his bed, Nate didn't even bother to remove his banyan. He grabbed a pillow and hugged it to himself. He fought the tears as long as he could, but his heart shattering into tiny pieces inside his chest became more than he could bear. Staring at the wall, he allowed a few tears to escape.

He had loved and lost twice, and he didn't think he had it in him to take that chance ever again.

Chapter 10

The following morning, George let Tanner help him dress for what would be an important day. Not a happy one, if he was honest, but a necessary one. He resolved to ask Lady Lily to marry him. He knew he had the approval of her father, and it would be best that he did so and they could get on with their lives.

Nate's words still stung. If he intended to hurt him, he had. George supposed he couldn't blame him. He rejected him and refused to admit that he loved him. No good could come from doing so. It was better for Nate to move on and take a wife. The sooner they each accepted what their respective futures must be, the better. Perhaps George would miss him less one day. He hoped. Because living with his broken heart and knowing he had also broken Nate's almost made him question his resolve.

He shook off the notion. It was done. He would arrange to speak to Lady Lily after they broke their fast and get it over with. They could announce their betrothal at dinner, and she could start planning the wedding while he tried to convince himself to ditch his sour attitude so he didn't make her miserable every day of their marriage. The least he could give her was that.

George entered the breakfast room and found Lady Lily already seated. Viscount Callan was at the sideboard. He recalled what Nate had said, and a pang of guilt hit him. But he reminded himself that if he asked her and she said "yes" that he had nothing to feel guilty over. If she declined his offer, he'd have to decide if he was going to involve her father or not. George would just hope it wouldn't come to that and she would accept him.

He added his selections to his plate and took the seat on her left, noting Viscount Callan seated himself on her right.

"You look well this morning, my lady," George said, working to capture her attention.

"Thank you, my lord."

"Might you do me the honor of a garden stroll after we finish our breakfast?"

She grinned at him, but it was of a friendly nature. Not one of love or desire. He knew very well what those expressions looked like, and she didn't love him. It was probably for the best as he would never love her either. He'd respect her and care for her, perhaps love her as a friend but not as anything more.

"Yes," she replied. "I would enjoy that."

He asked her about some of the plays she enjoyed, knowing that the conversation would keep her engaged. She mentioned to him last night that she had enjoyed attending the theatre and hoped to do so again soon. He had learnt a lot about her spending so much time in her presence yesterday in his attempt to avoid Nate.

He attempted to push Nate out of his thoughts again, but his entire body responded to the figure that entered the room. George didn't even need to look over at him to know that it was Nate. The house party couldn't end soon enough so that he'd hopefully never see him again. It was perhaps the only way his heart might finally forget about him. If such a thing were even possible.

George straightened his shoulders and fought to appear unmoved and unbothered by Nate's arrival. He focused on what Lady Lily said and ignored the reaction he had to the person he loved more than anything. He should have at least kissed Nate one more time. No, he told himself. That would only make matters worse.

What had Lady Lily just said? He smiled and nodded, hoping that was the appropriate reaction to whatever she explained about some Shakespeare or Stormy Wells play.

"Lord Knox," a male voice said from behind him, saving him from having to provide a verbal response to Lady Lily's conversation. He turned his head and saw the Duke of St. Albans standing on the other side of him, behind his chair. "Might I borrow a few moments of your time? I have an estate near your county seat and had a few questions."

"Of course, my lord. Give me just a moment," George replied. He turned back to Lady Lily. "I apologize, my lady. Will you meet me in the salon in a quarter hour or so?"

"I understand. I'll see you there. Take as long as you need."

She was understanding, at least. He wasn't certain he could handle being married to a wife who would nag him and maintain a state of displeasure.

George rose from his chair and followed the Duke of St. Albans to the library. The same library where Nate had kissed him for the first time. The memory would be etched on his heart forever, as much as he wished for it not to be the case.

He closed his eyes and pushed away the thoughts of everything else that had occurred since it would only cause problems for him to react to such memories in front of a duke.

"Are you all right, Knox?" the duke asked.

He drew a deep, fortifying breath and opened his eyes. "Indeed. What was it you wished to speak to me about?"

The conversation took way longer than George had expected. St. Albans wanted to know about crops and harvests in the area. He had inherited an estate in the area and wanted to see what would be the most profitable. He also wanted George's recommendation for an estate manager who knew the area, perhaps one of George's servants, who would be ready for an elevated position.

George found the duke to be an amiable gentleman. Not at all as stuffy and impatient as some dukes were reputed to be. He was someone George might even consider a friend if he were to spend more time in the man's presence. He said he would call at George's estate when he was in the area, so the odds of seeing him again were high.

He made his way to the salon, hoping that Lady Lily wouldn't be too angry with him for keeping her waiting.

Suddenly, he heard shouting and screams as gentlemen and servants hurried towards the back of the house. Without question, he ran towards the commotion to see what had happened. When he reached the exit at the back of the house, he was met by a cloud of smoke. He covered his mouth and nose and saw a side of the barn had caught fire. There were horses being led out by servants. A few cries for help came from inside. He took in the scene and continued closer to the barn.

The one side didn't look like it would hold out much longer and it was only a matter of time before the entire structure went up in flames. George heard screams from within the burning building and assessed how he might be able to help before he noticed another gentleman take off running inside the barn. Nate.

"NOOOOOOO!" George shouted, running to the entrance. It took every bit of a minute or more to reach the entrance. Several horses ran out and a couple of grooms came out after them.

"We were trapped, and he freed us," a groom said, coughing and collapsing against George. George slowed his fall to the ground.

"Where is he? Was there anyone else?" George shouted.

The man coughed. Beside them, one side of the barn caved in at the corner. George drew a deep breath and ran into the burning building. Nate was the kind of man who ran into burning stables to save people, and George damn well wasn't going to stand idle and not try to save him.

He moved quickly, doing his best to see through the smoke. He didn't hear anyone moving, and he didn't see any more horses or people. Nate hadn't come back out, so he had to be inside there somewhere. Adrenaline and desperation to find Nate kept him moving deeper into the building.

He saw an arm on the ground through the smoke and rushed to it. His heart knew it was Nate. When he reached him, he was face down, coughing. He was attempting to crawl out and quickly losing oxygen from being surrounded by the smoke. Nate collapsed completely onto his stomach, and George wasn't certain if he was still breathing.

George didn't waste a moment and clasped his arms. He pulled and dragged him towards the entrance. He just focused on each step, knowing that Nate's life depended on George's ability to pull him to safety. Damn him for running into the barn and risking his life. It was courageous and brave, but if he died, George knew he couldn't go on.

The other back corner of the barn caved in on itself and a burning pile of wood fell where Nate had collapsed. The need to save the person he loved most in the world coursed through his entire body and George found another burst of strength, pulling Nate at a faster pace. Once he was close to the opening, he called for help. A couple of gentlemen ran to him, and each looped one of Nate's arms over their shoulders and carried him out.

George took the last few steps out of the building and collapsed to his knees on the ground, coughing and tears rolling down his cheeks. He fought to get more air into his lungs, coughing up the smoke. St. Albans ran to him and helped him stand, moving him away from the burning building just before the rest of it collapsed on itself. George coughed and continued to work the air back into his lungs.

"Where is he?" George finally got out between coughs.

"Breathe, Knox. You need to get your breathing back to normal. You took in a lot of smoke."

George gripped St. Alban's shoulders. "Where is he?" he asked again.

"Demming? I'm not certain."

There was a crowd of people just outside of the house, and George took off running. He heard someone shouting for everyone to back up and give them room. He pushed through the crowd and saw Nate lying on the ground.

Lord Callan tried to pull him back while Lord Ockham's butler was blowing air into Nate's lungs. Ockham turned Nate to his side and patted Nate's back as Nate's breathing was shallow and barely visible.

Ockham wiped his brow after he shifted Nate to his back.

"Don't you dare stop," George barked out at them.

"Knox," Ockham said, sadness thick in his throat.

"No, goddammit. He ran into that barn and saved the others. You save him right fucking now."

A few of the onlookers gasped at George's outburst, but he ignored them all. George dropped to his knees beside Nate and moved him back onto his side.

"Knox, you hardly have your breath back. Move. Let us do this," Ockham said, shoving him to the side to hold Nate in place.

The butler blew air into Nate's mouth, and Ockham pounded Nate's back. George didn't move from his knees beside Nate, willing him to breathe. Believing that if he breathed enough air into his own lungs, he might be able to breathe enough for the both of them, and Nate would survive this.

George dipped closer to the madness with every second that Nate's eyes remained closed and his breathing shallow.

The man blew another burst of air into Nate's mouth and George drew his own breath when Nate coughed. Ockham patted Nate's back, helping him to cough up all the smoke that had been in his lungs.

George fought the tears that threatened to fall. The whole house party had already witnessed his outburst and the last thing he and Nate needed was for them to read anything further into the reaction.

George moved so he was in front of Nate and could see his face. He hated how Nate looked pained every time he coughed but was relieved knowing that each cough meant that he could breathe and he was filling his lungs with much-needed air.

Ockham helped Nate to sit up, and he finally opened his eyes. Nate looked around until his eyes landed on George. George looked back at him, wishing they were alone so he might wrap his arms around his neck and then yell at him, telling him to never put himself in danger like that again. Then kiss Nate senseless as soon as he was confident the man could breathe.

"Can you say anything?" Ockham asked, capturing Nate's attention.

"What happened?" Nate asked, his voice hoarse and barely above a whisper.

"You were the first to arrive and saved the rest of the servants and horses inside. Then he"—Ockham nodded to George—"ran in after you and dragged you out. He saved your life. Thank God."

Panic marred Nate's expression. "Are you certain everyone made it out?" The man had nearly died and then asked about the well-being of others. George's heart swelled with pride at just how good of a man Nate truly was.

"Yes," Ockham assured him. "Everyone is accounted for. The horses, too."

Relief washed over Nate's face, and he coughed a couple more times.

"You both need to rest after such heroics. I am in your debt for certain." Ockham turned to speak to a couple of his footmen. "Please help Lord Demming and Lord Knox up to their chambers, then send for their valets."

Two men approached and helped Nate to stand. George rose beside him. Nate waved off their help to walk and took a few steps on his own. "I don't need help upstairs. Just send for Thompson," Nate said, his voice still hoarse.

"I'll walk with him," George said.

The pair entered the house and walked in silence for a few moments. Glad to be away from the scene outside with the entire house party staring at them.

"I'm sorry," George said, breaking the silence once they reached the stairs and knew no one had followed. "It's not good enough. You deserve better, but I'm so sorry. I was wrong about everything."

Nate didn't say anything but gave him a small smile.

"I don't expect your forgiveness," George said softly.

"We can discuss things when we are alone."

George wasn't certain if that was a good or a bad sign, but he would have to wait to find out. After what he had put Nate through, he deserved as much. George swallowed hard.

"I don't mean to make you suffer. I just can't kiss you right now," Nate whispered as they reached George's door. "Knock when all is clear."

George shook his head. "No, your valet will want you settled in bed as you should be. Unlock the door now, and I will listen there. Clap several times when it's clear and I will come to you."

Nate nodded and continued on to his chamber without looking back. George opened his own door, and Tanner appeared only a few moments later.

A half hour passed, and George had undressed and had the tea and light repast that Tanner insisted upon. He knew the man wouldn't leave him alone until he did, and he didn't want him returning to collect the tray.

Once Tanner finally left, George locked the door behind him. He crept to the adjoining door and listened. George would stand there as long as it took until Nate signaled for him.

He wasn't sure how long he had waited, but he finally heard Nate's claps. His heart pounded, and he slowly opened the door, peeked his head in and saw Nate sitting on his bed, leaned back against a pillow with his blankets up to his waist. He had nothing covering his torso, and he took George's breath away. How he thought for a second he could live without the man, he wasn't certain. He was the fool.

He immediately went to Nate's door to lock it, hoping Nate hadn't troubled himself to get out of bed to do so. Once the door was locked, he turned to face Nate.

"I'm really sorry," George said. He wasn't certain he could ever say it enough times.

"So you said."

"I was a bacon-brained idiot."

"I quite agree." Nate didn't appear angry, just a bit of amusement in his expression.

George wasn't mad at his statement. He had every right to agree and to call him much worse.

"I also love you."

"You love me and want to figure out how we build a life together or you love me, but you are going to pretend you don't?"

George flinched. The question stung, but he knew he deserved it, and Nate was right to ask. At least he was certain Nate didn't doubt that George loved him.

"I want a life with you. I can't live without you. If you had died…" George's voice trailed off, and his heart was in his throat.

"No one understands that better than me," Nate said, his eyes glassy.

George swallowed hard and went to him, knelt on the floor beside the bed and took Nate's hand in his. "I am so sorry I caused you even a minute of pain after what you had already been through. I feared what might happen to you if anyone found us out. The other gentlemen were talking about men like us, and the things they said were hateful and vile. I just thought it might have been easier." George drew another breath and wiped away the tears that fell to his cheeks. "But if I have to live with only seeing you certain days and months out of the year and loving you in secret, that is better than not being with you at all. I love you. Please forgive me."

Nate pulled him to sit beside him on the bed. "Stop apologizing. I was hurt, but I knew you were scared and believed you were doing the right thing." Nate's lips curled into a smirk that made George's heart do somersaults. "I would have given you some space, and then I would have made you see reason. You, my dear earl, are mine."

George leaned forward and pressed his lips against Nate's. His heart soared and his body hummed when Nate wrapped his arms around him and deepened the kiss. Their tongues danced, and the kiss was one of love and need, marking each other's soul with their unspoken commitment to love each other.

Nate broke the kiss and pulled back just enough to gaze into George's eyes. "Lord George Knox, will you marry me?"

Chapter 11

N ate watched George's expression shift to one of confusion, and he fought not to laugh at him.

"What? You know such a thing isn't possible," George replied.

"Who says it isn't?"

"Every vicar in England, the law, all of society, the very people downstairs regaling each other with the stories of us both running to a burning building, just to name a few. Do you require more?"

Nate loved watching George wave his hands about.

"You just listed the reasons we can't legally or publicly wed. I am asking if you are willing to make vows to each other that we will spend our lives together. To vow that we will figure out how to navigate this life and decide our future together. I don't need to sign a register to uphold the vows and promises I make to you as your husband."

George appeared to contemplate what he said, and Nate enjoyed watching his mind work.

"You're right."

"And as I have said before, I usually am."

George kissed him, and Nate would be a lucky man if he did so every day for the rest of their lives.

"I wish to marry you," George finally said, biting his bottom lip, which only sent a rush to Nate's cock.

"Well, you shall make me the happiest man in all of England." That was an understatement.

"When do you wish to marry?" George asked.

"How about tomorrow? I don't want to mar our happy day with all that occurred today. We can both think about what we'd like to say and promise to each other. And then do so right here."

George laughed. "Perhaps we shall be the first couple to marry in bed."

"It will make the bedding far easier," Nate said, pulling George to him to kiss him again.

George was the one who broke the kiss that time. "As much as I want to anticipate my vows with my betrothed, all you get after what occurred is me lying in bed with you. Watching you appear almost dead before me, I willed for you to take the air from my lungs. I won't risk you overexerting yourself before we are certain you are well."

Nate scooted over further on the bed. "Remove your banyan and get in," he said, patting the bed beside him. "I will agree to your conditions for today, but I make no such promise tomorrow."

"Very well."

George removed the banyan, and Nate instantly regretted agreeing to such a request. His cock stood proudly, and he smirked, seeing that George was equally affected. He'd have to get creative to convince his love that they deserved just a bit of pleasure.

George crawled into the bed, and Nate pulled him against him and placed kisses along his jaw and neck. "Does it count as exerting myself if you do all the work?" Nate whispered in his ear.

George's hard cock jumped against his thigh, and he knew the man was contemplating what he said.

"I suppose not. What did you have in mind?"

Nate pulled him on top of him. "Straddle me."

George placed a knee on each side of his hips, so he straddled him, their cocks brushing against each other.

Nate put his hands behind his head, ready to watch what George would do. "Stroke yourself."

George fisted his cock, and Nate's own shaft twitched. He bit his bottom lip, watching George make long slow strokes, leaning his head back, enjoying himself.

"Tell me what you are thinking about," Nate ground out, his voice gravelly.

"You," he said, releasing a small mewl, "inside my arse."

The urge to flip George over on the bed had never been stronger, but he would uphold his promise and know that he was going to do that very thing tomorrow.

George used his other hand and began stroking Nate's cock. Nate drew a quick breath and thrust himself into Nate's hand.

"Now, my future husband," George chastised. "That is crossing the line into exerting yourself. I shall have to take you into my mouth if you don't stop."

Nate responded by thrusting himself into George's hand again.

"Very well." George shifted so that he settled between Nate's legs. He sucked Nate's entire length into his mouth and Nate's eyes rolled to the back of his head. George moved his mouth up and down on his shaft, licking and sucking.

Nate opened his eyes and looked down to watch. George shifted so his hand went between his legs. "Yes," Nate said, encouraging him. "Fuck your hand while you suck my cock."

George moved his hips to rock into his hand and sucked Nate's length all the way to the base. He moved his mouth on his length a few more times and Nate filled his mouth with the warm proof of his climax. George swallowed all of it and thrust a few more times into his hand before he groaned and spent on the bed.

George removed himself from the bed and returned with a cloth to wipe away the mess and tossed it aside before climbing back into bed.

"You are going to rest now," George said, his tone offering no negotiation.

Nate wrapped his arms around him and encouraged him to settle in close. "We both are."

The next morning, Nate woke up with George's back pressed to his front. He had his arm draped over his waist. His cock became aware of their position, and he tamped down the desire to take him right away. The next time they coupled, it would be after they said their vows and formed the marriage of their hearts.

They each took trays in their room the previous evening and didn't return to join the other guests. After what had occurred, their hosts wouldn't be offended that they each wished to rest. They would do the same thing for breakfast and make an appearance downstairs later. George had the idea for them to each inform their valets they would sleep in and didn't wish to be disturbed until they rang for them.

Nate relished that they shared a bed and had the privacy of the morning together by themselves. George moved and every part of Nate's body was aware.

"Nate," George whispered, turning over to face him, wrapping his arm around Nate and rubbing his back.

Nate leaned forward and placed a tender kiss on George's lips, then nuzzled his neck. "Are you ready to marry me? I can't wait much longer."

"Very much so."

"Well, come on, then," Nate pleaded, climbing out of bed. He pulled George to the edge of the bed.

George shook his head and laughed but shifted his feet to the floor and joined Nate.

"Should we dress?" George asked.

"No. Everything I am is laid bare before you, just like this."

George wrapped his arms around him and kissed him with such need that Nate's knees sagged. Nate allowed the kiss for a few moments and then stepped back. "Vows first, then all the pleasure you can handle."

George bit his bottom lip in response, and Nate's cock jumped. Nate clasped his hand and dragged him to stand just beside the window, then pulled the drapes back so the morning sun shone on them. The light gave George's hair a touch of golden glow and his cheeks were flushed. He had never looked more handsome or more tempting. And George would be his.

"Please allow me to go first. You'll say something so perfect, I shan't compete," George said, clasping Nate's other hand so they stood before each other naked, both hands held between them.

Nate nodded, urging him to speak.

George drew a deep breath and stared into his eyes with nothing but tenderness and love.

"Nathaniel Baring, I didn't realize just how much I lacked a part of myself until I found you. You have made me feel whole, as well as loved and treasured. It is you who I wished for when I didn't even know what I wished. What I vow to you is to go through every aspect of our lives together, working through any challenges we face together. I vow to love and cherish you and remain true to you for all our days." George's voice caught on the last few words, and Nate wiped away a tear from George's eye with his thumb.

He continued to cup his cheek and gazed into his eyes, swallowing hard to find his words.

"George Knox, I can't promise you what the future holds, nor predict what difficulties may lie ahead. What I can vow to you is that as long I breathe, I will ensure you are safe and loved. I vow to be by your side and do everything in my power to give you the life you deserve. I also vow to love and cherish you and shall remain true to you for all our days."

Nate shifted the hand on George's cheek to the back of his neck and pulled his mouth to him, their kiss sealing their promises to each other. Nate pulled back and grinned at him. "How does it feel to be a married man?"

"Is it actually official if it hasn't been consummated?" George asked, reaching between them and gripping Nate's cock.

Nate drew a breath and pressed his lips to George's again, backing him towards the bed. He swept his tongue into George's mouth and tasted every bit of him. He sucked George's tongue into his mouth, massaging his tongue against it until George gripped his shoulders and groaned, sagging against him.

Spinning George around, Nate pulled George against his body, then sucked and licked on his neck from behind. He'd never tire of the salty taste of his skin. George leaned his head back on Nate's shoulder, giving Nate better access to continue marking his neck with his mouth.

Nate ran his hands down George's sides, massaging his way to George's hips. He gripped them and pulled George's arse harder against his throbbing cock, teasing himself. He shifted a hand to George's front and took his cock in hand.

George moaned and thrust himself into Nate's fist. Nate kissed his way up to George's ear. "You are so fucking hard," he whispered, increasing the pace as he stroked George's cock.

"I want you," George whimpered between moans.

Needing no further invitation, Nate released him and stepped to the dresser and pulled out the oil. He returned to George and resumed his position behind him, giving him a couple nibbles on his neck. "Bend over the bed, love."

George eagerly did as Nate commanded and bent over, resting his elbows on the bed, and his arse on display for Nate. His forever. Nate massaged the cheeks of George's bottom, his perfect creamy skin and soft moans almost more than Nate could handle.

He opened the jar and dipped his fingers inside, coating them. Carefully, he pressed two fingers inside George's warm, tight hole. George pushed back against him, trying to take his fingers deeper.

"Eager, are we?" Nate teased.

"I'm ready. I want your cock."

Nate fucked him with fingers a few times, licking his lips at the muffled sounds George made, attempting to keep from being heard.

He withdrew his fingers and dipped them into the oil again to coat his cock. He stroked himself a few times, his cock harder than the finest steel with anticipation. Nate closed the jar and tossed it to the side of the bed.

Gripping George's hips, he positioned himself at the puckered opening and slid himself inside, coming more undone inch by inch until George had taken all of him. He withdrew and thrust back inside, all the way to the hilt in a single fluid motion. He saw stars burying his cock inside of the man he loved. His husband.

George shifted forward, then pushed himself back hard against Nate's front. Nate stilled and watched him repeat the action a few more times, taking his own pleasure from fucking Nate's cock with his arse.

"You are begging to be fucked, husband," Nate said.

"And what are you going to do about it?"

Nate placed both palms against the small of George's back, pushing him to flatten his chest against the bed, angling his arse just a bit higher. Nate immediately thrust hard into George, who had his mouth covered to prevent the entire house from being made aware of the ecstasy taking place behind their walls.

Nate thrust hard and fast. Each thrust one of love, one of possession, one of joining together forever. He watched his cock move in and out of the perfect arse before him, attempting to record to his memory everything about their first coupling after promising themselves to each other.

Everything about Nate's movements was primal, pounding, and needy. He pushed hard to hold George in place, knowing his climax was coming.

"Nate," George moaned. "I'm going to…"

Nate became unhinged by his words and drove into him harder. When George cried out, biting down on his hand, Nate crested the pinnacle of his own climax as deep inside of George as he could be. Slowing his thrusts to ride the wave of the most intense release he had ever had in his life. When he could get his wits about him, he leaned forward and placed several kisses along George's back.

Carefully, Nate withdrew and went to the washbasin for a clean cloth, which he dipped into the cool water. George hadn't moved from his position, bent over the bed, and Nate chuckled at the sight.

Returning to George, Nate wiped the oil away from around his arse and helped him to lie on his side on the bed, so he could clean George's stomach where he had spent on himself. Nate then cleaned his cock and set the cloth to the side.

After climbing into the bed beside George, he kissed his forehead.

"I love you," George whispered, his eyes heavy when he grinned at Nate.

"I love you."

They lay together for a few moments, running their hands lazily along each other's bodies. Nate's heart swelled at the intimacy of it all and the affection between them.

"What will we do when we leave here?" George asked, worry crossing his handsome features.

Nate pulled him closer and wrapped his arms around him. "What if we travel for a while? We'll go somewhere where no one knows us, just two bachelors rutting around another country."

George pulled back from him. "Need I remind you that you are now a married man?"

"Well, that's our secret, and the only rutting I'll be doing is with you."

"When can we leave?" George asked, settling back against him.

"We must stay for the rest of the house party so as to not draw attention to ourselves. Perhaps a sennight after?

That should give us time to settle our estates and arrange our travel."

Pain marred George's expression. "I don't wish to be apart from you for a sennight."

"I know, love. We will be as quick as we can. We'll figure it out," Nate said, nuzzling his cheek against George's head, reassuring him. "Does this mean you won't be offering for Lady Lily now?"

"Shite. Of course not. I hope you are right about Lord Callan. The poor girl likely suspects a proposal from me is forthcoming."

Nate laughed. "As I say, yet again. I usually am."

Epilogue

2 YEARS LATER

George nudged Nate, trying to wake him up. They had stayed up far too late the evening before, and George's cheeks flushed at the memory. They had been married and blissfully happy for over two years and still couldn't get enough of each other. Their intimate life had only gotten wilder and more passionate the longer they were together.

"Nate, you must wake up. I shall need to depart soon."

Nate tightened his hold on George. "No."

George laughed. "You know I must, and then we shall break our fast together."

Nate's eyes blinked open and the tender smile he gave George upon seeing him made George's heart melt as it did many times every day.

There was a light knock from the adjoining parlor to their bedchamber. "Just a moment," George called out. He climbed from the bed and wrapped his banyan around himself, tying it closed. He grabbed Nate's and tossed it to him. "Hurry and put that on, Handsome."

Nate groaned and shifted his feet to the floor, picked up the robe and put it on as George instructed.

"You may enter now," George called out.

The door swung open. "Sarah is waiting for you," Mary said.

George sighed. "I'm going there now." He gave Nate a quick kiss on the lips and nodded to Mary as he exited their chamber and crossed the parlor to the adjoining chamber.

"Good morning," Sarah called out, grinning at him. "You don't look like you got much sleep."

"I hope the coffee is ready when we get downstairs. Nate and I shall each need our own pot."

Sarah laughed and patted his arm. "Are you ready for me to ring for Tanner and Tilly?"

George nodded and stepped to the window of the chamber and glanced out at the vast estate of Nate's country home. It was already a beautiful day, and George would ask Nate to go on a walk with him after breakfast.

He shifted his attention back to Sarah. "Did you and Mary sleep well?"

"Better than you two, it would seem. Even though we're both a bit uncomfortable and sleep doesn't come as easy these days."

George glanced at her rounded stomach. It would only be a couple more weeks and the babe would be here.

"If there is something we can do to make you both more comfortable, you shall have it. All you need to do is speak the words."

She rubbed her stomach and grinned at him. "I know. You both have been very attentive. Mary and I are taking good care of each other."

George and Nate, by a twist of fate, met Sarah and Mary during their travels. Nate had saved them from an attacker, fortunately, before any harm had come to either of them. They came to learn that Sarah and Mary were in a similar situation to George and Nate's. Once they reached their majority, they convinced Sarah's spinster aunt to travel so they could leave and have a better chance of loving each other without the eyes of the *ton* on them.

They had all become close friends and hatched the plan to wed so they might have a chance at a contented life back home in England. It was well known that Sarah and

Mary had been close friends for years, so it was expected they'd wish to visit each other often with their husbands in tow.

They all moved back and forth between Nate's and George's primary estates. The servants likely found it odd that each couple always insisted on putting the other couple in the same suite, staying in either the countess or marchioness chamber, but as far as the staff was concerned, each couple was a besotted love match. It wasn't exactly untrue. They made it clear to their staff that their dearest friends should always have the best accommodations they could offer.

The sharing of the suite also made it easier to switch rooms for them all to dress and go about their day. It wasn't the simplest of arrangements and required a lot of coordination, but it minimized the sneaking around they would have to do otherwise and ensured they minimized the nights spent apart from their true respective spouses.

George hated the nights when they weren't in the same house. To keep up appearances, they didn't always arrive on the same day when it was time to change houses to tend to the other estate's business. It would appear odd if the couples didn't spend some nights in their respective homes without guests. It would become even more difficult when their children were born, but they would make it work. There wasn't a day that went by where George wasn't certain and assured of Nate's love for him. They always figured things out together, along with Sarah and Mary, just as Nate had promised.

They had all agreed that they wished for children, but it took a couple months of planning to attempt the effort. They all had many conversations about how they would pull off the endeavor, and where each person would be in the process, and what their role would be. All four of them were a part of every step of the process, each couple ensuring the well-being of their respective true spouse. It wasn't the most comfortable experience for any of them, but they all deemed it worth the effort. Sarah and Mary tracked their cycles to give them the best chance of conception, since the act was a matter of necessity and not one that anyone wished to do more than was required.

Nate and George decided together that Nate would father both babes, thus making them siblings. George didn't give a whit if the babes were biologically his. They would be a piece of Nate, which would make him love them just as much as he would have loved a child if he had sired them himself. Part of him found it amusing that if Sarah gave birth to a boy, his father's title, which he valued above all else, would be carried on by a child not of his blood.

Sarah showed signs of increasing after the first month, while for Mary, it wasn't until the second month's attempts that they were met with success. They hadn't decided if there would be any further children, but all hoped that these two would be brought into the world safely. Sarah and Mary had become their closest friends, which was ideal given their living situation, and the men worried equally for their health during the delivery.

An hour later, they had all broken their fast. The men helped the ladies make themselves comfortable in the drawing room where Sarah wanted to read while Mary worked on her embroidery. Once they had them settled, Nate pulled George towards the stables.

"I thought we might go for a walk," George said.

"I want to take you to the hunting cabin," Nate said, wickedness in his expression. It was their private place for the two of them where they could escape on "hunting trips" and be alone without all the pretense required in their daily lives.

They had their horses saddled and took off across the field until they were out of sight, then slowed. Nate trotted up beside George on his horse and matched his pace.

"This may be our last trip for a while," Nate said.

"I agree. Sarah could have the babe soon." A bit of worry panged at George's insides.

Nate must have noticed. "Are you all right, handsome?"

"I just hope the women and babes are healthy."

"All will be well, love." Nate grinned at him, and every smile from his handsome face had the power to make all of George's fears crumble, at least for a while.

Something about Nate's smile reminded him of the night they had stargazed together at the house party. They had snuck out to do so countless times since then, but that first time would always be his favorite, and the memory he held dear in his heart.

"What did you wish for that night? When we drank wine from the bottle and ate day-old bread?" George asked.

Nate stopped his horse, and George did the same. He shifted his horse so they were right beside each other and Nate could reach him. Nate reached out and cupped George's cheek with his hands, then placed a soft kiss on his lips before capturing his gaze again.

"This. All of this. A life with you."

Want more of Nate and George?

They have appearances in the other books in the Unlikely Betrothal series! If you haven't read book one, *The Earl and the Vixen*, get your copy today: https://books2read.com/theearlandthevixen

Here is a look at the full series, and keep reading for a sneak peek at the next book, *The Viscount and the Wallflower*, which will feature Lily and Alex!

The Unlikely Betrothal Series

A different couple at the same house party finds their match! Who will be next? Each of these books are stand-alone stories complete with a HEA and lots of spice, but recommended reading order is below:

Book 1: <u>The Earl and the Vixen</u>

Book 2: <u>The Rake and the Muse</u>

Book 3: <u>The Marquess and the Earl</u>

Book 4: <u>The Viscount and the Wallflower</u>

Book 5: <u>The Duke and the Widow</u>

Dearest Reader

Thank you for taking the time to read *The Marquess and the Earl*! I hope you enjoyed this spicy read, which is the third book in my Unlikely Betrothal series. I enjoyed bringing Nate and George's story to life on the page and can't wait to introduce you to the other couples at the Ockhams' house party!

I am so thankful for all my readers and would appreciate it if you would leave an honest review on sites like Amazon, Goodreads, BookBub, etc.! Also, I'd love to stay in touch, so please visit christinadianebooks.com to join my mailing list and receive a free copy of Only A Rake Will Do (the Ockhams are in that one, too!), and stay informed on upcoming releases, promotions, and current projects.

If you are interested in being on my permanent ARC team and/or Street Team, send me a message on one of my socials! I'd love to chat!

I hope all of you will follow me and get the latest happenings and info on releases from my historical romance friends on any of my socials:

- Website: christinadianebooks.com

- Instagram: @christinadianeauthor

- Facebook: christinadiane

- TikTok: @christinadianeauthor

- YouTube: @ChristinaDianeAuthor

- Twitter: @CDianeAuthor

- GoodReads: ChristinaDiane

- Follow Me on Amazon: Christina Diane

- Follow Me onBookBub: Christina Diane

- Join my Reader Group: The Swoonworthy Scoundrels Society

Hopefully I left you wanting more, so keep reading for a sneak peek at what is coming in *The Viscount and the Wallflower*, book four in the Unlikely Betrothal series! I hope you are as excited as I am for Lily and Alex! You can also go ahead and get your copy of *The Viscount and the Wallflower* here: https://books2read.com/theviscountandthewallflower.

The Viscount and the Wallflower

LONDON, ENGLAND - SPRING 1813

L ady Lily Fairfax braced herself for her mother's discerning eye as she descended the stairs of her parents' opulent London townhouse to attend her first ball out in society. She had made her bow before the queen, marking her as an eligible debutante on the Marriage Mart. So Lily would do as she was expected and she would attend the season with the intention to make an advantageous match with a gentleman of the highest title. At least that was what her father expected of her. Her father was an earl and preferred his daughter to marry a man of the same station or higher, but at a minimum a titled gentleman was expected.

Lily was nothing but practical and she knew she wouldn't be the type of lady that the pompous men of the *ton* wanted for their wife. She much preferred time spent reading a book or play as opposed to household matters, and she didn't have even the slightest interest in the latest fashions. If that weren't enough, her unfashionable red hair and light smattering of freckles on her nose and cheeks weren't what was considered beautiful in the eyes of society. Then, when you added her gold-rimmed spectacles, which she needed if she were expected to see far away without everything turning fuzzy and blurry, she would be overlooked for one of the more fashionable beauties seeking a husband.

So, in her mind, it went without saying that she would not command the attention that a diamond of the first water would, or even as much as the debutantes a few rungs below that. Lily figured it was their loss as she quite liked the way she looked. When she looked in the mirror, she just saw herself, a lady who loved the written and spoken word, had a sharp wit, and understood the way of the world from watching it. She couldn't look like or be anyone but herself, even if that meant she would end up a spinster, to her father's disappointment.

If nothing else, she had her books and her plays. The thing she most looked forward to about being out in society was going to the theatre, so she might see some plays she had read so much about. She was enamored with the display of passion and emotion from the works that she had read, particularly from Shakespeare. Stormy Wells, a torrid playwright who had taken society by storm, was all abuzz in the news sheets. She hoped she would get to experience one, or all of them, for herself.

As Lily made her way down the last few steps to meet her parents, her confidence wavered. It was one thing to feel confident in one's own home, but was quite another to be out in society where everyone seemed to have opinions and rules for everything. It baffled her how their society lived by a system where women were property and pompous men continued to decide what was acceptable behavior for all. How convenient that it was acceptable for men to attend brothels and keep mistresses, but women must be pure and devoted to their husbands.

"Lily, really?" her mother called out. "Give me the spectacles."

"Mama, don't you wish me to be able to see the gentlemen?" Lily knew it was too much to hope that her mother might ignore them. She should have tucked them in her reticle and then put them on once they arrived.

"You will see well enough without them. And you can make use of your quizzing glass if the need presents itself."

Lily huffed and tucked her spectacles in her reticule, hoping that would appease her mother. Her parents meant well. They cared about her, she supposed, but they were products of their society. They cared most about titles and social standing. Lily's younger brother would be the next earl, and it was her responsibility to marry well to further the family's connections. Or some such shite that Mama had told her more times than she cared to count.

"There, much better," her mother said. "Perhaps we should have powdered your hair."

"We must leave if we don't wish to sit in the carriage for an hour from the traffic," her father said, tapping his foot as he checked his pocket watch. He wasn't the kind of man that one typically said "no" to. When he wanted something, he typically got it, either by intimidation or throwing money at them.

For once, her father's impatience would work in her favor. She would much rather cause a scene in their foyer than have her hair powdered. It wasn't like the gentleman who married her wouldn't find out she had vibrant red hair.

They departed and boarded their carriage with no further primping and assessing of Lily's assets. At least, that's what her parents believed were her assets. She would argue that her ability to read and comprehend any text with ease, memorize plays, and to speak multiple languages would be assets, but what did she know? Nothing, it would seem in the eyes of society, which was certainly more their problem than it was hers. Not that anyone cared she thought so, as she wasn't the one who made the rules.

Once they arrived at the Fletchers' ball, they greeted their hosts and then were announced into the ballroom. She collected a dance card, and then her mother helped to place it on her wrist. There were fans fluttering everywhere from the other young ladies on the Marriage Mart, excited for the first ball of the season. Lily fought not to laugh at the display and wondered how effective the fans were in catching a man's attention.

She followed her mother to where some of the other matrons had gathered. She had already met all of them when they visited during the calling hour, so she offered her best curtsy when they greeted her. They spoke of some of the beautiful debutantes and who they believed would make grand matches. It wasn't lost on her that none of them deigned to compliment her appearance. Not that she required their hollow words, but she would have thought social protocols might have warranted as much.

The entire evening passed by at a snail's pace. Not a soul asked her to dance, and she wondered if she had somehow disappeared from view for all the gentlemen since they didn't glance in her direction either. Although she supposed she didn't bother to acknowledge them either.

Her mother made a few introductions, but each gentleman had to speak to someone about a matter of import, or something of the like. They could at least get more creative with their excuses to escape her presence without asking for a dance. Mama simply reminded Lily that she needed to smile and appear approachable as if she were the one who did something wrong.

If she put all her self-worth on how popular she was within society, she would be at rock bottom by then, throwing herself onto the floor with no will to go on. But she was her own source of strength and contentment and used the time spent ensconced against the wall, pretending to watch the dancers while she did a few complex calculations in her head and recalled some of her favorite Italian poems from memory. When it was time for supper, she mentally acted out a few of her favorite scenes from *A Midsummer Night's Dream* in her head while she ate. She was reciting some of Puck's lines to herself when her mother informed her they were ready to depart.

They wouldn't stay for the rest of the ball. Thank God for small favors. She flashed a victorious grin at her mother and then followed her parents out to wait for their carriage. Once they had settled into their squabs, she knew it was only a matter of time before one of her parents commented on her lack of success, so she stared out the window and waited.

"Did you meet anyone of interest?" her father asked.

"She didn't dance a single time," her mother said, her tone one of annoyance and contempt. Again, making it appear as Lily's fault that a gentleman didn't ask her to dance.

"Not at all?"

She almost took it as a compliment that her father was surprised. Then she thought that she should contemplate what a sad state of affairs that was.

"If you don't catch a man's interest during the season, I will make an arrangement," Papa said, confirming that there was no compliment intended.

"I am sure I will meet someone at the next ball," Lily lied. She just didn't want her father to play matchmaker or her mother to get any ideas about powdering her hair again.

The next few balls were much the same. Lily dressed in the most fashionable dresses, according to her mother, and spent her evening as a wallflower. Worst of all, in her mind, was that she had made no friends. The other debutantes either didn't take notice or perhaps wished to avoid catching whatever misfortune they believed had landed her on the wall.

She fiddled with her spectacles as she watched the dancers at Lady Harrowby's ball and recalled lines from Hamlet that evening. She glanced down the hallway that was within her view from her place alone and saw a handsome gentleman appear from one of the rooms, adjusting his cravat as he returned to the ballroom. A couple of seconds later, a blond woman appeared from the same room and caught Lily's eye as soon as she emerged.

Lily's eyes widened, not sure how to react. The woman smirked at her and started straight for her. Lily swallowed hard, trying to decide what she would say. Did she pretend she didn't witness them leaving their tryst in the middle of a ball?

The woman came to stand by her side. "You can keep a secret, can't you?"

"What secret?" Lily asked, giving her a knowing look.

"Exactly," the woman said. "I don't believe we have met."

"Lady Lily, the Earl of Fairfax's daughter," Lily said, giving a small curtsy.

"Lady Preston," the woman returned. "But I shall call you Lily, and you shall call me Rosina. Friends can dispense with the formalities, can they not?"

Lily wasn't sure that witnessing the woman's dalliances made them friends, but she wasn't in the position to turn down even the hope of having someone interesting to talk to.

"Of course," Lily replied. "If I had the luxury of disappearing for a while, I might do so. These things are rather dull."

Rosina laughed, then snapped her hand over her mouth. "I thought I was the only one. Do you see the way these debutantes act like this is all they live for? It makes me quite glad that I married and didn't have a season."

Lily's eyes grew wide at the realization that Rosina had a husband.

Her new friend noticed Lily's reaction and spoke again quickly. "My dear husband passed away. I have decided that I am open to making new…acquaintances."

Lily noticed the pain in Rosina's eyes. "I am very sorry about your husband," she said, offering her a small smile.

She thought a subject change might serve Rosina well. "Perhaps that is why I haven't danced a single time this season. Not enough fan fluttering, I imagine. Is the flutter supposed to wave the gentlemen to them?"

Rosina laughed again and gripped Lily's arm to steady herself. "You are far too interesting for any of these idiots. Well, not all of them are so bad. I shall introduce you to the best people of the *ton* to befriend."

Lily cringed as her mother approached.

"Lily, stand up straight," her mother admonished, then positioned her shoulders where she wanted them. "And try to smile, dearest. You want to appear approachable."

"Mama, have you met Lady Preston?" Lily said, hoping her mother would realize she was being quite rude not addressing her.

Her mother realized her error and Lily almost laughed at the light shade of pink that reached her mother's cheeks. "My apologies. I'm not sure where my head is. It's so taxing with a daughter on the Marriage Mart. It is good to see you out of mourning, my lady."

"Thank you, my lady. Your daughter and I have become fast friends. She is one of the most lovely young ladies out this season."

Lily fought not to laugh at her mother's reaction, unsure what to say in response to such a compliment to Lily.

"Indeed. She is sure to find her match soon."

Lily knew her mother didn't believe that in the slightest. To her good fortune, one of the matrons waved her mother over, and she excused herself.

"Your mother is quite overbearing," Rosina sympathized.

"You didn't have to compliment my appearance, Rosina. I am far from the beauty these titled gentlemen shall set their caps at."

Rosina pulled Lily's arm so that she faced her. "None of that talk. You are unique and quite beautiful. I imagine that red hair of yours is quite eye-catching in the sun. Don't let anyone compare you to the young misses who all look the same. When you meet the right gentleman, he shall take notice, and you shall be the only person he will ever have eyes for. Who cares if you dance with one or a hundred gentlemen? Only that one shall matter."

Lily decided not to point out that it was easy for Rosina to say such things when she had blond hair and perfect skin—and had already been married once before.

"I shall think about what you said."

"You just need to be around others that appreciate you. You appear more approachable when you are afforded the opportunity to be yourself. I am going to make sure you are invited to the Ockhams' house party at the end of the season," Rosina said, clasping her hands together in excitement. "I'll convince your mama to let me be your chaperone. We must get you out of these dreadful ballrooms."

Lily would enjoy the opportunity to be away from her parents and perhaps meet other interesting people. "I would appreciate that if it isn't too much trouble."

"Nothing is too much trouble for my friend. And now you will have me to spend time with at these events." She paused and glanced around them. "When I'm not otherwise engaged."

"Is it too forward for me to ask questions about your…engagements? Mama won't tell me anything about what to expect when…" Lily let her words trail off, assuming her friend would understand her meaning.

A playful smile appeared on Rosina's lips. "I shall answer any question you wish."

"I am going to hold you to that. Perhaps we shall take tea together soon."

"I'm going to attend the theatre tomorrow. Would you like to join me? Your mama might let you attend without her since I am eligible to be a chaperone. You could join me for dinner at my townhouse and then we could attend together. It would be so much fun."

Lily fought to keep from letting the depth of her excitement show. Going to the theatre with a friend would be an absolute triumph compared to the insincere pleasantries and forced enthusiasm of yet another tedious London ball.

"That would be wonderful. I believe *Duke About Town*, the newest play by Stormy Wells is playing, is it not?"

"You are correct. Do you follow the theatre?" Rosina asked.

"I do as much as I can, but I've never seen a performance before. It would be such a delight to see one of Stormy Wells' plays."

Rosina looped her arm in Lily's. "Then come with me to find your mama. I will arrange everything."

Lily might not have succeeded in landing a husband, but as far as she was concerned, the season was looking up.

Acknowledgments

There are so many amazing people in my life who have supported me, new and old. Authors and readers! I truly appreciate each and every one of you and hope that you will continue to stick with me on this journey. I would like to call out a few key people, but please know that this isn't an exhaustive list and there are so many people whom I love and adore. I wish that I had room to name them all!

Steve: My husband is the one who continually supports my big and daring dreams, all while providing tech support, cooking dinner, doing the laundry, spitballing ideas with me, and so much more! He's a true partner in every extent of the word and I couldn't do any of it without him. Love you, Babe!

Dexter and Felix: My boys frequently provide me with distractions while I'm in the middle of writing. However, they are also often the inspiration for some of the witty sibling banter that makes it into my drafts. I don't even know what they're going to think when they realize one day that their mother writes smut. Oh well… I love you, boys!

Rachel, Nina & Brittany: I am fortunate to have these ladies (my mom, aunt, and sister) in my life. They have been there for me the entire way and have supported me through the ups and downs throughout the years. They are all used to my crazy ideas and what I can do when I put my mind to something. They just keep cheering me on. They are the ones who hold all of my embarrassing stories and memories, so I can't ever let anyone speak to them without me present. But I love you, all!

Erin: We were destined to be besties from our very first meeting. She is the person I talk to about all the things when I need to bounce around ideas, work on my mindset, take a breath, and so much more! Love you, dearly!

Morgan: None of this could be possible without her keeping the trains moving! If there is something with this biz that needs to get done, she is right there at my side helping move it forward, and she usually comes up with a simpler, better idea! Truly, thank you!!!

Bliss: I can't believe the good fortune we had to have met in a smutty follow train group on Insta, but here we are! It was another fateful moment! I would be sad without our daily texts, talking about our writing progress, smutty scenes, and all the happenings in life. Thank you so much!!!

Courtney: Fate struck again, and I am so thankful to have a partner in crime and twinsie for this author journey! Thanks for all of the ideating, chats, and feedback into the wee hours of the morning! We are going to rock this thing!

Thank you to everyone on my Beta, ARC, and Street Team! (Especially Rachel W., she has literally read every single word that I have written, and I haven't scared her away yet!) The love and care that you put into reading, providing feedback, and helping promote the stories means so much more to me than you know. I hope we get to keep hanging out together for many years to come!

Thank you to Dragonblade Publishing for seeing something in me and my stories! I know I am going to continue to grow in my author career with your guidance and support.

Thank you to all of the amazing author friends and influencers I have met through various social media groups!

This amazing community has seriously been one of the best parts of this whole journey, and I am thankful you all let me be a part of it!

About the Author

Christina Diane is an award-winning author who loves to write super spicy, fast paced stories set in the Regency era for the modern reader! If you love all the steam, witty banter, spirited heroines, and hot regency men...and can forgive a bit of creative liberty within the historical setting without expecting 100% historical accuracy, then you are in for a treat! She is a hybrid indie and traditionally published author with Dragonblade Publishing. While she does read a ton of Regency romances, she is also an avid reader of dark romance and thrillers.

She lives in Northern Maine with her husband and two boys. Her family also includes their three French bulldogs who go everywhere with them, as well as two solid black cats. The entire family is always up for new adventures.

When she is not writing or chasing after her family, she usually has a Kindle in her hand!

Her writing journey began at the age of nine when she created her own comic strip, Grizzly Grouch. In adulthood, she was a freelance writer for several years, mostly writing lifestyle pieces for blogs. She found that she couldn't stop thinking about stories and characters, so much that she had to get them on the page! Christina frequently has dreams of random character ARCs that go into a massive list of planned writings. She currently has more than ten series just waiting to be written!

Aside from her family, writing, and books, she loves Bridgerton, the Grinch, Jessica Rabbit, horror movies, Chucky dolls, cold brew, yoga, Hamilton, the color pink, and speaking in obscure quotes from movies and TV shows.

Christina loves chatting with her readers and talking about great reads, so please contact her on socials! She'd love to hear what you think about her books and what you'd love to see more of!